Submarine Warriors
The Enemy Beneath

ROB TIFFANY

Hood Canal Press

DEDICATION

This book has been extra-special for me because it involved my kids and even their friends. Writing the rough draft of a chapter and reading it to your children as a bedtime story is a wonderful experience. It's also the best way to get feedback from your target audience to ensure that it reads with the voice of a middle-grade boy or girl.

Thanks to Mike, Nick, Caroline and my wife Cathy for being such an integral part of this book.

CONTENTS

ACKNOWLEDGMENTS

Many people and events in my life helped shape this novel. It began with the Sailors, Marines, and SEALs I served with as a Submariner in the U.S. Navy. Living beneath the waves for months-on-end while reading Tom Clancy, teaching myself how to program software, and running missile drills made a lasting impression on my life. In writing this middle-grade adventure novel, I received inspiration and feedback from friends, fellow writers, and my family. Hood Canal Press takes this idea from a Word document to something tangible and special for readers all over the world. Last but not least, Cathy and Kathy get an extra-big Thank You for all their help.

PROLOGUE

Deep beneath the frigid north Pacific, the ocean floor trembled as a pyramid-shaped structure emerged from underground. The glowing, crystalline tip of this otherworldly object revealed itself above the seabed. It illuminated the dark ocean depths, and the surrounding, near-freezing water began to boil. Hundreds of feet up, the surface bubbled and spewed water into the sky like an erupting volcano. Marine life scattered in every direction to avoid the intense heat projected from this underwater anomaly.

A large cruise ship was returning from a two-week Alaska voyage. Destined for the port of Seattle, it was about to leave the Pacific Ocean behind and enter an inland waterway called the Strait of Juan de Fuca. Without warning, the giant vessel rocked violently back and forth as it encountered an area of turbulent, bubbling water. Crewmembers and passengers alike were thrown to the deck as the collision alarm sounded. Many of the tourists relaxing in deckchairs suddenly found themselves thrown overboard into the boiling sea. The ship's compass spun wildly as loose metal objects flew violently through the air.

"Helm, give me a hard, right rudder and accelerate to full speed!" ordered the Captain.

"Controls are unresponsive sir," the Helmsman replied. "We can't navigate away!"

"Radioman, send out an SOS!"

Moments later, the ship tilted upward and plunged beneath the churning waves, entombing thousands of innocent people.

The White House

"Mr. President, I need you to take a look at this." The Chief of Staff entered the residence to wake him up. "Twelve hours ago, one of our satellites picked up an unusual heat signature from the Pacific Ocean off the coast of Washington State. Some of our scientists think it's an underwater volcano, but we don't know for sure."

The groggy, young President sat up and turned on his bedside lamp, glancing at the clock. "Darren, nobody mentioned anything about sleep deprivation during the campaign. Why do I need to know about an undersea volcano in the middle of the night?"

"Sir, an overdue cruise ship never made it home to the Port of Seattle." The Chief of Staff dropped a classified folder on the President's lap. "Its last known GPS coordinates were in the vicinity of the heat disturbance."

"I suppose the two of us didn't get much sleep during our Delta Force days in Afghanistan either. Go drag the NSA and the Joint Chiefs out of bed and meet me in the Situation Room in thirty minutes," the President ordered his longtime friend.

CHAPTER 1 > THE MISSION

Subase Bangor

Cold, Pacific Northwest drizzle added to the tearful scene on the Delta pier as crewmembers from the USS Alaska said goodbye to their wives and children. The gray skies seemed to blend in with the dark water and black submarines. One hundred and eighty sailors from the Blue Crew were departing for a seventy-day strategic deterrent patrol. Alternating Blue and Gold crews ensured continuous operations for America's Trident fleet. With twenty-four submarine-launched ballistic missiles each, professional submariners kept their nuclear arsenal at-the-ready in order to deter other countries from attacking the United States.

Captain Connery's twelve-year old daughter, Caroline, hugged him tightly. She knew it was almost time for him to lead his crew on another undersea mission.

"Dad, when are you going to get out of this submarine business?" a tearful Caroline inquired. "I've lived half my life without you around."

"This is my last patrol, I promise. After this, I'm accepting an Admiral's post here at the base. We'll see each other so much you'll get sick of me."

"So you'll finally be an Admiral like Granddad?" Caroline smiled.

"Don't sound so surprised."

"I'm happy for you, but this better be the last patrol," retorted Caroline. "Don't make me come after you. I've got super powers, you know."

Just down the pier, the Alaska's Weapons Officer, Lieutenant Wyatt, bumped fists with his son Nick as he crossed the gangplank onto the flat missile deck of the sub. "I expect you to take out all the aliens in Halo by the time I get back."

"You know it, Dad," Nick yelled back as he ran down the pier. "I can handle any creature or boss they throw at me."

Nearby, Mike found himself face-down on the pier with a grimace on his face.

"I keep telling you, those untied shoelaces are going to trip you up one day," Sonarman Timbers said as he helped his son off the deck.

"Sorry, Dad." Mike looked up. "It's always dark when I get up for school and my eye-hand coordination isn't at its best when I'm tying my shoes."

Petty Officer Timbers pulled a plastic glow stick off his life vest and put it in Mike's hand. "The next time you need some light, just bend this tube, and it will start glowing brightly."

"Thanks Dad."

"Hey Mike, give me a ping," laughed Annie as she walked by with her best friend Chrissie. "Without my dad the Quartermaster, you bubbleheads wouldn't know where to go."

"Oh yeah, well, without my dad, the Alaska would be flying blind." Mike gave the girls a quick comeback.

"Without the Radioman, the sub wouldn't receive emergency action messages," Chrissie chimed in. "You'd be cut off from the rest of the world without my dad."

"I'd like to see your dad climb outside the submarine and fix a radio antenna while submerged," shot back Mike.

"Enough arguing." Sonarman Timbers broke things up. "Your dads are all important and we've got to get this show on the road. We'll see you back here in a few months."

The somber group of officers and men made their way down the escape hatches into the large ballistic missile submarine. The families and loved ones of the men who wore silver and gold dolphins on their chests consoled each other as they headed back to shore from the triangular Delta Pier. It's a scene that's been repeated hundreds of times since America began guarding its shores by patrolling the ocean depths with her most powerful weapon.

"Hey Caroline!" shouted Nick. "Let's get everybody together and meet at my tree house. I think everyone's safely below decks by now."

"Sounds like a plan. I'll text the others and see you guys over there." Caroline climbed into her mom's Suburban.

Once the last man dropped below decks and closed the remaining open hatch, the Officer of the Deck picked up a microphone and barked, "Station the maneuvering watch."

The crew scrambled to man their posts in preparation for getting underway. The idea of getting almost two hundred men from their bunks to their assigned stations in less than five minutes is easier said than done. The cramped quarters, narrow passageways, steep stairs, and small watertight doors of a submarine pose quite a few challenges to a sailor trying to get somewhere fast. Thanks to years of training, the engine room, torpedo room, missile control center, sonar shack, maneuvering, radio room, and control room were all manned and ready to go with seconds to spare. The Captain, Officer of the Deck, and two lookouts were stationed up in the sail to lead the way as the eyes and ears of the sub.

USS Alaska

It might come as a surprise to know that submarines require the help of tugboats when navigating through rivers or narrow channels and when arriving and departing from a port. This time was no different as a large tugboat, tied to the port side of the Alaska, gunned her engines to pull the submarine away from the pier.

"Ahead one-third," the Captain called down to the Helmsman driving the sub.

"Ahead one-third, aye," replied the Helmsman as he twisted the Engine Order Telegraph to the right.

Back in the Maneuvering section of the sub, the one-third bell rang. This alerted the nuclear engineer on watch to apply enough steam to the sub's turbines to attain the requested speed, the slowest. The Petty Officer gradually moved the large wheel to release the steam created by the nuclear reactor, and the propeller shaft began to turn.

The USS Alaska made its way northward through the Hood Canal. Often mistaken for a river, the Hood Canal is the largest fjord in North America. Twenty minutes later, safety cross-arms were lowered on the Hood Canal Bridge to stop civilian car traffic. Built by the military, the Hood Canal Bridge was designed to open so submarines could pass through and reach the Puget Sound and the Strait of Juan de Fuca. The strait is basically a large, nautical freeway between the US and Canada where ships and subs travel from the Puget Sound to the Pacific Ocean. It's common to see cargo ships, oil tankers and cruise ships coming and going through this Inland Passage.

The submarine spent several hours transiting through the strait. This was a real treat for the sailors who were outside on watch in the sail. The beautiful Olympic Mountains lay to the south and Vancouver Island to the north. Finally, the Captain gave the word to move the bridge down from the sail and into the control room. The USS Alaska was emerging from the western mouth of the strait, and the Pacific Ocean was opening up before it.

"Something feels different this time," the Captain thought to himself as he stared at the never-ending horizon of dark blue water. "You've got to keep it together for the sake of the rest of the crew." He gazed one last time at the lighthouse at Cape Flattery on the port side of his sub. With a final puff on his cigar, he climbed down the ladder and closed the hatch above him.

"Diving Officer, submerge the ship." The Captain dropped from the ladder onto the deck of the control room.

The control room is the nerve center of the sub and a very busy place. Here you find the Helmsman and Planesman who drive the sub, the Quartermaster who navigates, the Chief of the Watch who maintains the ship's buoyancy, the Fire Control Technician who launches torpedoes and missiles, the Diving Officer who maintains depth, and the Officer of the Deck who orchestrates everyone's activities.

At the Captain's direction, the Chief of the Watch called out, "Dive, dive!" on the 1MC microphone and then sounded the claxon.

Large vents on the hull of the sub opened and released air from the ballast tanks. Someone observing this from afar might mistake this for a whale spraying air and water from its blowhole. As the tanks filled with water, the Alaska became less buoyant and slipped beneath the waves to enter the Pacific Ocean.

"Dive, make your depth four hundred feet," the Officer of the Deck ordered.

"Make my depth four hundred feet, aye," replied the Diving Officer.

With that, the crew began its normal watch rotation for their seventy-day patrol. It was business as usual for America's latest generation of submarine warriors. One-third of the crew was on watch, and the other two-thirds were working, reading, playing video games, taking college courses, watching movies, or sleeping. Most were unaware of the secondary mission in store for some of their shipmates.

Captain Connery met with his senior officers in the Wardroom, a small room in front of the Galley where officers eat their meals and hold meetings.

"Gentlemen," the Captain called everyone to order.

"As you know, we have a secondary mission that will commence in a few hours from now. The logistics of this mission require us to rendezvous with the Navy's newest and most advanced Deep Submergence Rescue Vehicle, the USS Omaha Beach. It's currently waiting for us, one hundred nautical miles off the coast of Washington State and is manned by a single pilot. The Weapons Officer and three senior Petty Officers representing sonar, radio, and navigation will be joining me for this operation. When we transfer to the Omaha Beach, the Executive Officer will be in charge of the Alaska and it's his job to keep her safe."

The Captain glanced at the XO with a wry grin. "I'm not really sure what we're getting ourselves into here. All we know is that a cruise ship disappeared in the same area where our satellites detected an unusual heat anomaly coming from the bottom of the sea. Some think it's a new Bermuda Triangle and others speculate it's an underwater volcano. XO, I'm preparing for the worst, so I want you to keep the Alaska at a safe distance while monitoring our activities."

"So how will I know what a safe distance is, Captain?" asked the XO.

"Stay ten miles away and monitor us with passive sonar. The Omaha Beach will send you continuous telemetry data via High Frequency Internet Protocol (HFIP) so you'll always know our status. If things start to go badly for us on the Omaha Beach, I want you to get the Alaska out of harm's way at flank speed. Mr. Wyatt, assemble the rest of the team and meet me at the aft escape trunk in thirty minutes. We're adjourned here."

USS Omaha Beach

Out of the murky darkness of the North Pacific, a bright, silvery object slowly converged on Alaska's position as it arrived at the rendezvous point.

The Omaha Beach represented a radical departure from deep submergence rescue vehicles (DSRV) of the past. Looking more like a futuristic space ship than a miniature submarine, the Omaha Beach boasted its own small nuclear reactor to provide it with years of electricity and propulsion. The steam from its next-generation reactor could spin its propellers fast enough to achieve submerged speeds in excess of 100 knots. This enabled it to outrun almost any of the world's fastest torpedoes. Its flexible, titanium-composite hull allowed it to reach depths greater than 5,000 feet below the surface. Rather than having a giant bubble of glass in the front to see out of, the Omaha Beach was covered with tiny sensors and cameras. What appeared to be a wall of glass to anyone inside the sub was really a flexible Organic Light Emitting Diode (OLED) display designed to replace the typical forward viewport. This was safer than glass and allowed other information to be layered on top of the underwater view. Crewmembers could make hand gestures in front of the display to move pictures, text, video and other items from one part of the screen to another.

The Omaha Beach attached its docking collar over Alaska's aft escape trunk with a thud. Captain Connery spun open the hatch and greeted the Omaha Beach's pilot. The rest of Alaska's away team made their way into the high tech sub and manned their respective stations to begin the mission. The pilot undocked the DSRV from the Alaska and it began to hover. Quartermaster First Class Love entered the coordinates of the mysterious heat anomaly into Omaha Beach's navigation system.

"I heard the best minds from DARPA and US Navy research created this sub." Captain Connery surveyed the interior of the sub with the amazement of a child.

"Yes, sir," replied the Pilot.

"Then it's time to show me what this thing can do. Pilot, make best speed to our target."

Everyone felt themselves pushed back in their seats as the sleek Omaha Beach quickly accelerated to 100 knots and raced towards its destination.

Radioman First Class Grant created an HFIP link with the Alaska to send her telemetry data about vital systems and the surrounding environment. "Wireless is online," Grant announced to the rest of the team. "Everyone can now remotely control their stations from their personal devices and communicate with the Alaska via Voice over Internet Protocol (VoIP), instant messaging and email."

"Knowing my daughter Caroline and all your kids the way I do, I've got to believe they would love this futuristic sub," the Captain remarked to the rest of the crew.

"I second that!" Petty Officer Love had an excited look on his face.

"It's nothing short of taking command of the Millennium Falcon or the Starship Enterprise," added Petty Officer Timbers.

"I've never travelled at 100 knots per hour underwater before." The Weapons Officer pointed at the digital speedometer. "I'm sure our kids would think they'd made the jump to light speed."

A short thirty minutes later, the Omaha Beach closed in on the source of the heat signature. The sub's compass moving erratically was the first clue that something wasn't quite right. To make matters worse, the DSRV began to be pulled downward by an invisible force.

"Captain, I'm losing depth control," exclaimed the Pilot. "At 100 knots per hour, this should be next to impossible. I've got the diving flaps on full rise - with no effect. "

"Everyone run a full diagnostic test on all ship's systems," the Captain ordered.

"All systems nominal," reported the team members one by one as their results were displayed.

"All stop," barked Captain Connery to the Pilot.

"All stop, aye," the pilot replied.

As the Omaha Beach's forward movement slowed, its downward momentum increased dramatically.

"Radio, send a distress signal to the Alaska and the Commander of the Pacific Submarine Fleet!" the Captain exclaimed.

THE OMAHA BEACH HAS ARRIVED AT THE
COORDINATES OF THE HEAT ANOMALY
AND IS BEING PULLED TOWARD THE
BOTTOM OF THE OCEAN.
DEPTH CONTROL IS LOST.

The message quickly went out to the Alaska and was routed to COMSUBPAC in Pearl Harbor via Extremely Low Frequency radio.

"Omaha Beach, this is the Alaska. What's your current status?" the XO asked over the underwater connection.

"XO, we are accelerating toward the sea floor and it seems like there's nothing we can do to stop it. You should be receiving our complete ship's status via the telemetry feed."

"It doesn't make sense, sir. We're seeing the data, and your sub is in perfect condition," replied the XO. "Everything we're receiving shows that the Omaha Beach is operating within normal parameters."

Suddenly, the various display panels around the DSRV began to flicker and show distortion.

"Omaha Beach, your telemetry readings are starting to break up." The XO's choppy voice echoed through the DSRV. "I'm no longer receiving your complete stream of data. I'm also noticing some inconsistencies between your ship's compass and the inertial navigation system."

SUBMARINE WARRIORS > THE ENEMY BENEATH

Unexpectedly, the sunken cruise ship appeared on the large display on the front of the Omaha Beach control room. Captain Connery spread his hands apart causing the image of the cruise ship to zoom-in and fill the entire screen. She appeared to be perfectly intact with no structural damage.

"Alaska, we've found the cruise ship on the bottom of the ocean."

"Copy that, Omaha Beach," replied the XO.

"I'm going to go out on a limb and speculate that there could be large pockets of air trapped inside the vessel." The Captain stared at the ship on the display. "If there's air, there could be survivors."

Suddenly, the crew of the DSRV felt periodic thuds, as the lifeless, floating passengers of the cruise ship struck the hull of their sub. They looked on in horror as they saw hundreds of bodies floating toward them as they grew closer to the sunken luxury liner. Most were disfigured and half eaten by sharks. All of them were wearing clothes that told the story of what they were doing just before realizing they were on the Titanic. A Hawaiian shirt on a shuffleboard player, swim trunks on a swimmer, an evening dress on a woman dancing, a silk shirt and gold chain on a high-roller, and a bikini on a sunbather.

"Oh my God, it looks like we're flying into an asteroid field of bodies!" exclaimed Petty Officer Love. "What could've caused all this?"

"It's like nothing I've ever seen or imagined," the Captain replied. "Whoever's behind this, they might be trying for a repeat performance with us. It feels like we're

15

being pulled toward the bottom by a tractor beam out of Star Wars, and I don't want us to end up like those poor souls floating outside."

"Captain, I'm picking up an increase in seawater temperature," said Sonarman Timbers. "Luckily, it's nowhere near the level of heat that was detected by the satellite or we'd be getting pretty toasty by now."

Suddenly, a giant, glowing pyramid revealed itself in the distance beyond the cruise ship. The water all around it shimmered in a distorted way because of the heat it was generating.

"What in God's name is that thing?" the Weapons Officer uttered.

"It looks like a glass pyramid sticking out of the seabed," replied the Captain. "There's some kind of radar or satellite dish next to it, as well. Sonar, send out a ping to determine our range to the unidentified target."

"Verifying range to target, Captain," said Petty Officer Timbers.

A loud, clanging sound enveloped the submarine as the Sonarman sent out the ping.

"Captain, we're roughly 5,000 yards away from the target. I can't get an exact reading because heat emanating from the pyramid has created a protective thermal layer."

"Very well," replied the Captain.

"One more thing, sir," the Sonarman added. "Our range to target is decreasing rapidly. It appears the tractor beam is reeling us in."

"Alaska, this is the Omaha Beach, do you read?" Captain Connery spoke into his headset.

"Omaha Be____ , th__ is the Al___," replied the XO. "Your sig__l is bre_king up. Telemetry read__gs are all ov_r the map. We see the im_ges of the glowing crystal. We have no intellig__ce data on this. Treat as host_le!"

"Whatever foreign power is behind this, we can't let the technology in the Omaha Beach fall into their hands," the Captain declared aloud. He began to feel sweat trickle down his neck.

"Weaps, plot a solution and fire a torpedo at that thing on the double."

"Captain, the fire control computer is unresponsive," responded the Weapons Officer.

"Not like this," the Captain uttered under his breath. "If we can't shoot this thing and we can't get away…"

You could hear a pin drop as the crew of the Omaha Beach looked at each other in stunned silence and disbelief. Everyone onboard knew what the Captain meant.

"Petty Officer Grant, send the following message to the Alaska and COMSUBPAC."

USS OMAHA BEACH CAPTURE BY
ENEMY POWER IS IMMINENT. BEGINNING
SELF-DESTRUCT PROCEDURE.

"XO, this is the Captain," Captain Connery announced into his headset. "All electronic systems onboard the Omaha Beach are behaving erratically. We're only a thousand yards away from the ocean floor near a crystalline pyramid structure and some kind of radar dish. We cannot let the top secret systems onboard the Omaha Beach fall into enemy hands. We will therefore scuttle the ship before all our systems fail."

Captain Connery paused for a moment.

"It's been the greatest honor of my career to serve as your Captain. Please tell my wife and daughter that they're the best things that ever happened to me. Have the Alaska depart the area at best speed so you don't share our fate. XO, you're the Captain now."

"Mes__ge recei__d," replied the XO. "Th__ ca_'t be hap__ing!"

"Weaps, quickly initiate our self-destruct procedure before it's too late," the Captain ordered.

"Aye-aye sir," responded the Weapons officer.

Back onboard the USS Alaska, the XO sprang into action. "Helm, make your course zero-nine-zero. All ahead flank cavitate! I don't care how much noise we make."

"Making my course zero-nine-zero, all ahead flank cavitate helm, aye."

Back in Maneuvering, the nuclear engineer spun the wheel as fast as he could to bring the Alaska to flank (top) speed without regard for the extra noise created by air bubbles from accelerating too fast.

The USS Alaska quickly departed the scene to avoid the inevitable shock waves that would come from a self-destructing sub.

Back on the Omaha Beach, Captain Connery spoke softly to his team. "I'm sorry, but you've got thirty seconds to compose a digital family gram and get it to the Radioman for transmission."

Everyone onboard the Omaha Beach turned to their computer screens and quickly typed farewell messages to their wives and children back home.

Quiet sniffling and even some whimpering could be heard in the control room.

"Did you father ever have to face death like this?" the Weaps asked the Captain.

"Admiral Connery was just a kid when he served on World War II submarines." The Captain looked him in the eyes. "But he faced death every day."

The Captain and the Weapons Officer removed special keys from around their necks and inserted them into the main control panel. They both turned their keys to the right and the Captain poised his finger over a large red button.

Petty Officer Grant quickly transmitted the digital family grams to the crew's loved ones. An electronic message seemed to be an expedient, yet horribly impersonal way to convey the death of a service member. Those unwelcome knocks on the door, so feared by the spouses of America's fallen heroes throughout many wars, will arrive long after the bad news is already known this time.

"None of you deserves this ending," uttered the Captain. "I'm so sorry…"

Captain Connery had trained his entire career to push a button that would rain down nuclear missiles on America's enemies. Now he was pushing a different kind of button that would extinguish his own life and the lives of his crew. "What am I doing?" he thought to himself. His hands shook violently as he depressed the glowing red button with his index finger.

An eternity seemed to pass on the Omaha Beach as crew members sat with their eyes closed and their hands over their ears. Slowly, one by one, each member of the away team opened their eyes to see if they'd made it to Heaven.

The sub had gone dark and there was no explosion.

"What happened?" asked the Weapons Officer.

"It appears that we've lost power," the Captain replied. "Without power, the electromechanical features of the self-destruct system can't set off the charges."

"Yes!" yelled out Petty Officer Timbers as he high-fived Petty Officer Love.

Sighs of relief and laughing began to spread around the room.

With a little more conviction than before, Captain Connery pushed the self-destruct button several more times, to no avail.

"Let's not get carried away with that button pushing, Skipper," said the Pilot. "You might accidentally get that thing to work."

"Being alive feels pretty good." A relieved Petty Officer Grant spoke out in the darkness. "I'm sure whatever happens next couldn't possibly be as bad as being blown to bits."

Just as the Omaha Beach was about to land on the ocean floor, the strange radar dish reversed its magnetic beam and pushed the DSRV toward the pyramid. The sub eventually settled down next to the glowing structure with its occupants shrouded in darkness, due to the electrical disruption from the magnetic beam.

An accordion-like tube extended from near the tip of the crystal pyramid. It reached out to the Omaha Beach, arched over the top, and sealed itself to the upper escape hatch. The sailors onboard watched in disbelief as the hatch slowly opened and an infrared light washed into the main compartment. Several humanoid creatures dropped through the open hatch and landed on the main deck with a thud.

They looked like astronauts in black, spacesuit-like outfits and helmets. Peering out at the sailors from behind the curved, glass face-shields were ultraviolet, glowing eyes.

This turn of events quickly put the crew of the Omaha Beach on the defensive and everyone took slow steps backwards away from the intruders.

"This was definitely not in the Navy recruiting brochure when I signed up." A nervous Petty Officer Love tried to make light of this new situation.

"I think we just made first contact with an Alien civilization," added the Weaps.

"If you want to live, you'll come with us and you won't try anything stupid," one of the strange humanoids announced to the group.

"I guess they don't come in peace," uttered Petty Officer Grant.

Without warning, the Pilot pushed through the group towards the Aliens. "I don't take orders from freaks like you!" shouted the Pilot. He hit one of the creatures over the head with a fire extinguisher, knocking it to the ground.

Without skipping a beat, one of the other humanoid creatures reached out and clutched the Pilot's face with its hand. Intense heat shot out from its fingers and seared his skin.

The Pilot screamed in anguish as his face began to burn. "You're killing him!" the Captain shouted. "Stop, and we'll do what you ask."

"It's a little late for that, Overworlder." The creature released his grip and the Pilot's lifeless body collapsed to the deck. "Consider yourself warned. Now get moving!"

"Oh my God, he's dead." The Weaps picked up the smoldering remains of the Pilot. "We can't just leave him here."

"Oh, you will," remarked one of the creatures with an outstretched hand.

The Weaps suddenly felt an invisible burning sensation, causing him to drop the Pilot on the deck. "Okay, okay, I'll do what you want," the sunburned Weaps muttered to the creatures.

The terrified crew climbed out of the upper hatch, and the creatures forced the sailors through a translucent tube into an opening in the pyramid. After walking down a short corridor, the sailors were pushed into an airtight compartment and sealed inside. Everywhere they looked, they saw the red glow of infrared lights being used for illumination. With the crewmembers locked in their new underwater prison, the humanoids removed their suits and helmets to reveal their bald heads, hairless bodies and translucent skin.

"You're being quarantined in this containment cell to ensure we don't become infected by your Overworlder diseases," barked one of the humanoid creatures.

"Who are you and what right do you have to capture our sub and hold us prisoner?" Captain Connery shouted.

"We have every right, Overworlder scum!" A new creature with an ancient Egyptian headdress emerged from the shadows. "Did you think you were the only intelligent life on this planet? Did you really think you had this whole place to yourselves? We've lived under the continents and the ocean floor for centuries. We were once like you until our ancestors were pulled underground several millennia ago when the waves of the Red Sea crashed in all around them. They believed they had descended into Hell. But our surviving forefathers learned how to thrive deep beneath the Earth's surface. Our advanced race adapted to this subterranean world in a way that none of the Earth's other primitive cultures ever could. Over the centuries, our bodies and eyes evolved to better suit our underground surroundings. Constant exposure to radioactive elements has mutated our genes so that we have the power to project heat from our hands. Today, we are one billion strong and we control the world beneath your feet!"

"Why show yourselves now, and why did you sink the cruise ship and kill all those innocent people?" Captain Connery retorted.

"That's simple," replied the Underworlder. "Your technology is becoming advanced enough to threaten our civilization. You may not realize it, but we've been closely monitoring you for the last hundred years. We've tapped your undersea phone lines and fiber optic cables. We've watched you create great societies and technologies, only to destroy them with greater and greater ferocity. I only wish your barbaric cultures would have wiped each other out by now. Like some kind of runaway virus, you keep multiplying and consuming all the Earth's resources. Your world and ours are linked by a few miles of rock and ocean and we want those resources for ourselves. To that end, we've decided that your civilization has forfeited its right to exist on this planet. Consider the dead Overworlders on the cruise ship your first casualties in this new war. But for now, I have something different in mind for you."

"Commander, begin the wrapping process on the prisoners!"

CHAPTER 2 > THE COVER UP

Arlington, Virginia

It was a crisp, early autumn morning at the Arlington National Cemetery. A procession of black limousines and Suburbans made their way through the main entrance and parked. Members of the Secret Service jumped out of their SUVs and ran ahead to the cemetery grounds to secure the area. Following them up the hill was a long line of family members, friends, a Navy Chaplain, the Secretary of the Navy, and the President of the United States. They were all there to say goodbye to the crew of the USS Omaha Beach.

The group finally congregated around six headstones engraved with gold and silver dolphins, the universal symbols for submarine officers and enlisted men everywhere. The headstones included the names Captain Robert Connery, Lt. Samuel Wyatt, Petty Officer Aaron Timbers, Petty Officer Richard Grant, Petty Officer Tom Love, and Warrant Officer Paul Thompson. Most ominously, engraved beneath each of the names was the word Lost. The gravesites contained no bodies of the dead to mourn on this depressing day.

Caroline's grandfather, retired Admiral Connery, performed a quick scan around Arlington Cemetery and noticed many headstones with dolphins and the word Lost engraved on them. "Most of these are from World War II sinkings by Japanese submarines and German U-boats," he thought to himself. "Probably a few covered-up, cold war casualties, as well."

The sounds of weeping and sniffling could be heard as the Navy Chaplain delivered his sermon. "Dear Lord, lift up these brave patriots and defenders of America so that they may experience your glory and serve you in Heaven."

"The Chaplain doesn't know, does he?" the President whispered to the Naval Secretary.

"No, he doesn't know anything," the SECNAV replied.

The Chaplain went on for a few more minutes and then closed his Bible to conclude his sermon.

"I can't believe Daddy's gone," Caroline cried. "I was just talking to him last week. He said he wasn't going to leave me anymore."

By now, Caroline, Nick, Chrissie, Annie and Mike were sobbing uncontrollably.

The SECNAV walked over and put his arm around Caroline. "Your father was one of the greatest submarine Skippers in the Navy, and a good friend."

"Don't say the word WAS," Caroline snapped and pushed him away. "The Navy took him from me and now I'll never see him again."

The President looked across at the children. "I can't begin to tell you how sorry I am for your loss. You should all be proud of your fathers. They were very brave and cared deeply about you and their country. It's regretful that they would leave us so soon due to a mishap on a research vessel. It truly tears me apart."

Standing next to Caroline, Admiral Connery glared at the President with eyes reflecting utter disbelief.

"Your fathers, husbands, and sons took time away from their lives as undersea warriors to conduct important scientific experiments designed to remove harmful CO_2 from the air we breathe," the President continued. "This accident was unforeseeable, and the flooding that occurred pulled the research sub to depths far beyond our reach. We may not be able to find them, but you'll always be able to visit this place to remember them."

At that moment, sailors in dress-white uniforms aimed their rifles in the air and gave the fallen submariners a twenty-one gun salute.

Afterwards, the sailors presented each widow with an American flag, neatly and precisely folded into a triangle. This pushed the women over the edge into even greater levels of despair.

The children placed wreaths on the empty tombs and spent a few more moments at the gravesites.

"I paused our Halo game, Dad," Nick spoke aloud. "It will be your turn to play Master Chief when you get back." He then placed an Xbox game controller on the Weapons Officer's gravestone.

Eventually, the solemn group slowly made their way back to their cars and headed to Dulles Airport for the trip home to the Pacific Northwest.

The White House

"You think they believed it?" asked the SECNAV.

"They don't suspect a thing," replied the President. "Don't think for a second that I take pleasure in being involved in something like this. Creating cover stories for bizarre occurrences was not in the job description when I ran for President. I'd hate to think that my own government would've done something like this to me if I'd died when serving in Afghanistan."

"What about the report from Alaska's XO that their sonar gear didn't hear an explosion when the Omaha Beach self-destructed?" the Secretary pressed.

"That data is inconclusive. They were headed away from the scene at flank speed and the explosion took place behind them in their baffles. Trust me, Charley Keller and the rest of the Alaska crew will fall in line and do their duty. This is too important."

"I'm bringing the Alaska home early." The SECNAV stood up to leave the Oval Office. "They'll return to Bangor next week so we need to get another Trident to cover their target packages."

"Give the crew a couple of days to decompress and then I want a full debriefing of what really happened out there," ordered the President. "I want to know more about the glowing pyramid from the video. We need to know what we're dealing with."

"Yes, sir, Mr. President," replied the Secretary of the Navy as he left the room.

Poulsbo, Washington

Located on the Kitsap Peninsula and situated between the Hood Canal and the Puget Sound, Poulsbo was home to many Trident submariners. Caroline and her friends lived and went to school there.

Driving around Liberty Bay in her mother's car, Caroline noticed the sign that greeted visitors to her Norwegian town, "Velkommen til Poulsbo." She was home after a long plane trip and ferry ride from Seattle, but it didn't bring her any solace.

"How are we going to live without Dad?" Caroline asked her mom.

"I don't know, darling. We'll just have to take it one minute, one hour, one day at a time."

After a sad week of staying at home with nothing to do but cry or zone-out playing video games, the children of the fallen sailors returned to school. Annie, Chrissie, Mike, Nick and Caroline were all in middle school and the fall semester had just begun. Their teachers gave them lots of breathing room as their emotions fluctuated between sadness and anger over what had happened to their fathers. The children didn't notice their friends' attempts to reach out to them in the hall between classes. They just numbly walked through a constant haze of despair.

Caroline stared blankly across the room while pretending to eat lunch in the cafeteria. Sitting alone at the table, she wondered where the strange, buzzing sound was coming from.

"Am I daydreaming? "

"Oh, my phone's on vibrate," she uttered aloud, snapping back to consciousness.

Her phone displayed a white number 1 inside the text messaging tile on the Start screen. She tapped on the tile to see what the SMS said:

"NOTHING IS WHAT IT SEEMS. UR FATHER &
THE OTHERS MIGHT STILL BE ALIVE @
LATITUDE: 47.81 LONGITUDE: -126.71. FIND UR
GRANDFATHER.
HE'LL KNOW WHAT 2 DO. XOXO"

Caroline's eyes locked on the message and didn't look away for the next several minutes.

"No phones allowed on school grounds." The cafeteria monitor abruptly pulled Caroline out of her frozen state. "Give me that phone!"

Caroline quickly ran to the girl's bathroom, where the male cafeteria monitor couldn't follow her. She closed herself in a stall to collect her thoughts.

"This has to be a prank," she said under her breath, settling down from the excitement. "How could anyone be so insensitive, sending me a text about my dad?"

Caroline sobbed quietly as she tapped the People tile on her phone and flicked her finger upward until she found

"Granddad" under the G's. She tapped the phone number under his profile picture.

"Admiral Connery speaking."

"Granddad, it's Caroline."

"How are you doing?" he asked.

"Not too good. I'm a little freaked out right now. I just received a text message saying that all our dads might still be alive. It gave me some GPS coordinates and told me to contact you."

"Do you know who it's from?" the Admiral asked.

"That's what's so weird. There's no phone number listed, just the letters SAT."

"A satellite phone," he thought to himself.

"The end of the message kind of creeps me out," Caroline continued. "It's the symbols for hugs and kisses. I wonder if it's from some kind of stalker."

"I'm sorry, Caroline; I'm not up on the texting lingo of your generation. What are the symbols for hugs and kisses?"

"XOXO," Caroline replied.

"I remember those symbols when I received Valentine's letters from your Grandmother. It's a long-shot, but it's possible that the one person in the world who truly knows if your dad is alive just contacted you through a satellite phone."

"Huh?"

"I think it's Charley Keller," said the Admiral. "He's the Alaska's XO and a man with undying loyalty to your father.

"Uncle Charley?" asked Caroline.

"Yes. Keep this to yourself. Gather your friends together - the sons and daughters of the lost sailors. Meet me at your friend Nick's tree house tonight at nineteen hundred hours. Remember, don't tell anyone."

Caroline couldn't stop herself from smiling. When she got home from school, she called Nick, Mike, Chrissie and Annie and told them they all had an important appointment to keep. And no, she couldn't tell them why.

Tree House

At the edge of the Hood Canal in Nick's back yard, a giant tree house was suspended twenty feet in the air connected to four Douglas Firs. Not an ordinary tree house; this place was big enough to hold a dozen friends with a high ceiling so even adults could stand upright without bumping their heads. Though constructed mostly of wood, on the inside it looked more like a miniature NORAD or NASA mission control.

Electricity made it possible to have all kinds of things inside like lighting, laptops, flat panel TVs, Wi-Fi, a small refrigerator and lots of charging Smartphones and iPods. Most of the power came from the solar panels on the roof, combined with small panels in the tops of the trees. The rest came from small windmills along the banks of the Hood Canal. The tree house was also full of special, high-tech light bulbs that projected a variety of wallpaper designs on the walls. They could also project text, images and touchable controls on any flat surface. Most everything about the place could be controlled by voice, camera input, or Smartphone apps. Frank Lloyd Wright would be proud of the architecture.

The kids began to arrive at 7:00 pm and made their way up the rope ladder to this special place.

A hidden camera above the tree house door scanned Annie's face to see if it recognized her as the daughter of Quartermaster First Class Love. Of course, recognizing her was only half the equation. She had to know something secret and convey it to the camera, if she wanted to get inside. She made special gestures with her hand that looked like the ones used to communicate with the aliens in "Close Encounters of the Third Kind." The door unlocked and opened. As she entered the tree house, the wallpaper changed to a full-motion scene of a tropical beach where Annie was playing with dolphins.

The rest of the kids made their way through the open door and sat at their seats in front of their work/play stations. Individual messages from IM, Twitter, SMS, Facebook and email were projected on each of the kid's tabletops by the special light bulbs above.

The daughter of Radioman First Class Grant, Chrissie flicked through messages from her friends with her finger, without ever touching the table.

Nick resumed wandering around a virtual wasteland in Fallout.

Suddenly, the projected wallpaper changed to the image of Admiral Connery standing at the bottom of the rope ladder.

"Nick," the Admiral shouted up. "I'm too old to climb this thing."

"Step onto the bottom rung of the ladder and hang on," Mike yelled down to him. Sonarman Timbers' son turned a virtual knob projected on his desk and a mechanical reel began to pull the rope ladder and the Admiral upward.

Once the Admiral arrived at the top, he entered the tree house through the open door.

"Hey guys, this is my Granddad." Caroline motioned to the Admiral. "He's here to talk to us about our fathers."

Everyone in the room knew Caroline's grandfather was a famous, retired submarine Admiral. One couldn't help but notice the statue of him at Subase Bangor.

"I hope you're not here to give us another pep-talk like those stiffs back in Washington D.C.!" Mike blurted out.

"No, I'm not," replied the Admiral. "What you're about to hear is Top Secret. Caroline, pass around your phone to let everyone see the text message."

Chrissie, Mike, Annie and Nick all took turns examining the message on the phone.

"This message is strange," Annie mumbled.

"The message is from the XO of the USS Alaska, and those GPS coordinates point to a location off the coast of Washington," Admiral Connery proceeded. "The XO has risked his career in the Navy to send us this message because he thinks your fathers are all still alive."

It took a moment for the news to sink in.

The Admiral popped a flash drive into a nearby PC, and an image of the Pacific Ocean appeared on the wall. He spread his hands apart and the scene zoomed-in on a location just one hundred miles off the coast of northern Washington State.

"This spot marks the GPS coordinates," the Admiral pointed. "Notice how they're due west of the opening to the Strait of Juan de Fuca? Your fathers' submarine would've transited directly toward that location on its way out to sea. If they're alive, then that's where they are."

Nick's eyes widened at the prospect that his dad might be alive.

"But we just got back from their funeral in Washington D.C." Chrissie had a confused look on her face.

"Yeah, the President said they were doing science experiments and had an accident," Mike chimed in. "The President of the United States wouldn't lie to us...right?"

"I checked the GPS coordinates the XO sent to Caroline and the location appears to be a popular place," the Admiral added. "A cruise ship with thousands of passengers disappeared there several weeks ago and no one can explain what happened. I still have a lot of friends in high places throughout the military, and they're telling me that our orbiting satellites have spent a lot of their time looking at these same coordinates."

"I don't like the sound of this," murmured Chrissie.

"Listen, I'm not here to have you second-guess the President, and I'm not trying to invent a conspiracy theory," the Admiral said. "But I don't think your fathers were conducting a science experiment. I think they were on a Top Secret mission to investigate the sinking of that cruise ship and something went wrong. Something the President can't talk about. The Navy and the government have already written them off as dead. Due to the compartmentalized nature of their mission, the Navy will never admit that your fathers may be alive and therefore won't try to find them."

"So they just made all this stuff up?" asked Annie.

"That's exactly what they did," replied the Admiral. "They told everyone a story about an accident during a science experiment with a research sub that conveniently cannot be found."

"So what are we supposed to do about it?" said Annie, looking incredulous. "We can't exactly call the police."

"You're right, we can't tell anyone what we know. We're going to find them ourselves."

"That's crazy," Mike belted out. "We're just kids."

"Yeah, how are we supposed to find our dads out in the middle of the ocean?" Chrissie asked.

"We're going to steal a submarine."

CHAPTER 3 > THE PLAN

Tree House

"Steal a submarine…," Caroline proclaimed, "…nice."

"I think we'll need to send in Master Chief to pull off something this big." Nick referenced his favorite video game.

"I'm sure the submarine we're borrowing will have a Master Chief onboard," the Admiral replied, with a perplexed look.

"I doubt anyone in the Navy has gone through the SPARTAN-II Augmentation Procedure," Nick added.

"So, what's the game plan?" Annie asked the Admiral, who was still looking confused at Nick's comment.

"Well, since I've never stolen a sub before, we're going to do like the Marines and improvise," the Admiral answered.

"Fake it till you make it!" Mike exclaimed.

"My contacts at the Pentagon tell me that the Alaska has cut short its patrol and will be arriving home tomorrow afternoon," the Admiral resumed. "We've got to get down to the Delta pier and make our way onboard the Alaska while most of the crew is onshore. You guys will have to help operate the ship. Just keep suspending your disbelief and you'll be okay."

"It sounds like an awful lot of things will have to go right for us," Annie commented.

"You have no idea," the Admiral remarked.

"In a nutshell, we have to take control of the Alaska and drive it to the GPS location given to us by the XO. Along the way, we have to navigate the sub up through the Hood Canal Bridge, through the Strait of Juan de Fuca and dive into the Pacific. Once we reach the coordinates, some of you will have to suit-up in deep sea diving suits, leave the Alaska and try to find your fathers in their DSRV or wherever else they may be."

"Sounds like mission impossible," Mike remarked under his breath.

"Maybe he thinks we're the Spy Kids or something," Annie added.

"Chrissie, please download and display the full blueprints of an Ohio Class submarine on the wall for us," the Admiral asked.

"Sure thing," replied Chrissie.

A moment later, a three-dimensional view of the sub appeared on the wall. The Admiral walked over and motioned his hands to separate the different parts of the sub onto different walls of the tree house. The Engine room slid to the wall behind him, the reactor compartment moved to the wall on the left, the missile compartment stayed put, and the forward part of the sub slid to a wall on the right.

"Take a look at these four large areas of the sub." The Admiral pointed at the wall. We'll have to proceed with the assumption that all of the Alaska's systems are operational and not in need of repair. I'll need one of you back here in the engine room to control the speed of the sub and keep an eye on all these moving parts. We don't need to worry about the reactor compartment or the missile house. The rest of you will be up front with me. Typically, a new sailor reporting onboard a sub would have up to a year to learn everything about the ship in order to get his dolphins. Unfortunately, you kids don't have that luxury."

The Admiral proceeded to go over blueprints of the Trident submarine with the kids and gave them a crash course on the different systems and how they worked. Each of the kids had some knowledge of their father's job onboard the sub, which was helpful.

"Helmsman, Planesman, Chief of the Watch, Diving Officer, Fire Control, Officer of the Deck, Sonar, Torpedoes, Radio, Quartermaster, Maneuvering," the Admiral barked out his checklist of vital stations.

"Knowledge of how to operate various aspects of the sub by everyone in this room won't be enough," the Admiral remarked. "We're going to need a sympathetic crew that's eager to help us rather than have us arrested."

"How do we know the Alaska sailors won't shoot us when we try to take over the sub?" asked Annie.

"It's a calculated risk," the Admiral replied. "I'm betting on the fact that the XO can influence some of the crewmembers. The fact that your fathers are their shipmates also works in our favor. It's critical that we get assistance from at least one of the watch sections if we hope to take the Alaska to sea."

"What's a watch section?" Chrissie asked.

"The crew of a submarine works on an eighteen-hour day," the Admiral answered. "The crewmembers are divided into three groups, or sections, that each work six-hour shifts. While section one is driving the ship, section two is watching a movie, reading a book or performing other tasks and section three is sleeping. Luckily, no one has to hot-rack on a Trident."

"Hot rack?" a puzzled Mike queried.

"On smaller, fast-attack subs, there aren't enough bunks for all the crew members," the Admiral explained. "Therefore, someone is sleeping in your rack while you're on duty."

"That's totally gross!" exclaimed Caroline. "I don't want someone else's drool on my pillow."

"Nobody said serving on a naval vessel was a pleasure cruise," the Admiral added.

Admiral Connery then ducked outside to the tree house deck where he made several very official-sounding phone calls on his cell phone.

In the meantime, the kids continued to study submarine schematics and manuals.

"Hey everybody," Mike exclaimed. "I need all of you to set the Wi-Fi on your smartphones and tablets to ad-hoc mode. This will give us a private, peer-to-peer wireless network onboard the sub where we can communicate with VoIP and send each other emails and documents. Set the SSID to Treehouse. Also, to prevent others from snooping, enable WPA2 security and set the passphrase to Seabeck. I'll be placing extra access points throughout the sub to make sure we have full coverage."

"I've converted all the ship's manuals to PDFs and the schematics to Visio diagrams," announced Annie. "You can grab what you need off my file share."

The Admiral hung up his phone and came back inside the tree house to address the children.

"Okay kids, here's the plan. I've talked to the Bangor subase commander and received approval to give you all a tour of the Alaska when she returns to port tomorrow. Because of everything you've been through, he thought it was a good idea to help give you closure. We won't enter the sub until all non-essential crew has come topside to the pier to greet their wives and kids. This will leave only the one-third of the crew that has to remain on watch to do things like power down the reactor and other systems."

"I sure hope they don't think we're non-essential," Mike said nervously.

"One more thing; the base commander also gave me permission to bring you to the dive simulator tomorrow morning before the Alaska returns," the Admiral said with a smile. "You're going to get a crash course in driving a Trident submarine. Now everybody go home and get some rest."

Trident Training Facility (TriTraFac)

After showing identification to the Marines at the main gate of the Bangor Submarine Base, the Admiral and the kids proceeded to the Trident Training Facility. It looked like an unassuming office building nestled amongst the tall Douglas Fir trees.

"Good morning everyone," announced Chief Petty Officer Gartrell to the gathered Admiral and children. "I can't begin to tell you how sorry I am about what happened to your fathers."

"Thanks, Chief," replied a sleepy Nick.

"This morning you'll learn how to dive and drive a Trident submarine like a pro," the Chief continued. "Here we have every aspect of the control room completely simulated using the most high tech gear you've ever seen."

"Is this like an Xbox?" Chrissie asked.

"Even better," Chief Gartrell replied. "Instead of playing a game on your TV, you'll be right in the middle of the action. Do any of you remember movies like Jurassic Park?"

"Sure, those dinosaurs rocked," Nick responded.

"The same Silicon Graphics technology used to make that movie is used here," the Chief added.

A giant simulator was supported in midair by hydraulic columns, allowing it to shift from the right to the left and pitch the bow up and down. It could simulate the calm feeling of gliding through the water at five knots, as well as the sudden shock of a collision. The Admiral and the kids entered the huge floating box to discover an exact replica of an Ohio-class control room. There were chairs and steering wheel-looking yokes for the Helmsman and Planesman, as well as control panels everywhere with colorful flashing lights.

"Admiral, why don't you be the Officer of the Deck for this exercise?" Chief Gartrell spoke as he walked behind the control panel.

"I'd be delighted," replied the Admiral.

"Annie and Chrissie, you two sit in those chairs so you can pilot the sub," the Chief directed. "Annie, as the Helmsman, you'll steer the sub to the port and starboard, and you'll dive and rise by pushing the yoke forward or pulling it back toward you. You also have the job of controlling the speed of the sub by twisting the engine order telegraph - that's the knob over there. You will take your steering and speed orders from the Officer of the Deck and your depth orders from the Diving Officer."

"Chrissie, as the Planesman, you'll control the ship's bubble or pitch by pushing down or pulling back your yoke. You'll take your orders from the Diving Officer.

"I feel like I'm sitting in a 787 cockpit." Annie giggled as she sat down next to Chrissie.

"Mike, sit over there and man the Chief of the Watch station." The Chief pointed to a panel to the left of the Planesman's station. "You will bring water into and send water out of the sub to control buoyancy. You'll also be able to move water fore and aft to keep the sub level or to help the Planesman with the angle of the sub."

"Nick, go sit over there and man the fire control panel. You will plot firing solutions based on the speed and bearing of your submarine, as well as that of your adversary.

You'll flood torpedo tubes, open and close the outer doors and fire wire-guided torpedoes when ordered."

"You mean these torpedoes have actual wires attached to them?" Nick asked.

"That's correct," Chief Gartrell replied. "Thousands of feet of wire is spooled out of each torpedo allowing you to remote control it from the sub. Once the torpedo is near its target, you can have it go active and begin pinging to home-in for the kill."

"That's so cool!" Nick exclaimed.

"Caroline, I want you to be the Diving Officer," the Chief continued. "You will stand behind Chrissie and Annie, and it's your job to achieve and maintain the depth ordered by the Officer of the Deck. If we're at periscope depth, it's your responsibility to ensure the ship doesn't broach the surface. When the Officer of the Deck orders you to make a particular depth, it's your job to get there smartly."

"Smartly?" Caroline repeated with a perplexed look on her face.

"Quickly," translated Chief Gartrell.

"Alright everyone, we better get to work if you ever want to be trusted with a two billion dollar submarine," the Chief barked, as he walked behind the computerized control panel. "Man battle stations!"

The kids spent the rest of the morning learning how to steer, dive and surface a sub on the simulator, using planes, a rudder and high-pressure air. They even got to react to a simulated torpedo attack and a close-aboard explosion and lived to tell about it.

Finishing up their training just before noon, the children thanked Chief Gartrell, piled into a Suburban with the Admiral, and drove back to Nick's house.

Tree House

Chrissie was the first one out of the SUV and climbed up to the top of the rope ladder upon arriving at the tree house. When the door opened, her eyes opened wide in surprise as she gazed into a fully occupied tree house.

"Mom?" Chrissie gasped as though she'd been caught red-handed doing something wrong. She looked back at her friends below. "We are so busted."

As it turned out, the moms of all the children were inside the tree house waiting for them - and that's not all. Their mothers had already filled backpacks with breakfast bars, laptops, water bottles, phones, snacks and other supplies for each of the children.

"This is so not happening," Mike sighed.

"Time for lunch," announced Nick's mom. "You're going to need your strength in order to take part in an important mission like this."

"How did you know about this; and how come we're not already grounded?" asked Nick.

"I told them last night." Admiral Connery spoke up. "We need their help to pull this off. They won't be with us on the Alaska, but they have other important and risky tasks to accomplish."

"Granddad, I don't want them involved in anything that could get them in trouble with the Navy," Caroline protested.

"Speak for yourself," Caroline's mother Julia retorted. "Your fathers are our husbands. If there's even the slightest chance that they're still alive, then there's nothing we won't do to try to get them back."

"Listen, everyone," the Admiral spoke. "This is going to be an extremely dangerous mission and there's probably more that can go wrong than any of us have considered. If we're successful in stealing the sub, the entire US Navy will be coming for us. In order to save your fathers, we'll probably find ourselves leapfrogging Osama bin Laden on America's Most Wanted list.

"The SEALs already capped him," Nick pumped his fist in the air.

"Right. Regardless, the President won't take kindly to having his gold watch stolen."

"Gold watch?" Annie looked puzzled.

"The Trident submarine is the most powerful weapon that the President has at his disposal," the Admiral replied. "It's sometimes referred to as his gold watch."

"Oh," Annie nodded.

"Listen, I don't have a sword or any sand to draw a line in, but I want you all to know that you don't have to participate in this endeavor," the Admiral continued. "You're all very smart and very brave and I see a lot of your fathers in each of you. If they could see you now, I know they would be very proud. Once we start this mission, though, there's no turning back. It's unlikely you'll ever be able to return to your old lives as normal kids in school."

The Admiral paused to let the gravity of his words sink in.

"If you're with me, I want you to come over here and put your hand on top of mine."

The Admiral reached out his hand.

"I'm with you, Granddad!" shouted Caroline, as she sprung to her feet and placed her hand on top of his.

"I'm with you too," said Nick, placing his hand on top of Caroline's.

"Me too!" yelled Chrissie, running over to place her hand on top of Nick's.

One by one, the rest of the children and all of their mothers rushed over to place their hands on top of each other's like a football team in a huddle.

"Go Panthers!" Caroline yelled out evoking their Poulsbo Middle School mascot.

"Yeah, go Panthers!" Mike echoed.

"Panthers! Panthers! Panthers!" everyone chanted excitedly as they streamed out of the tree house toward an uncertain future.

CHAPTER 4 > STEALING THE SUB

Subase Bangor

After cruising southward through the Hood Canal, the USS Alaska pulled up alongside the Delta Pier with the assistance of a tug boat.

"Helm, all stop," ordered the XO.

"All stop helm, aye," the young Helmsman replied.

With that command, a Petty Officer back in Maneuvering spun the giant wheel to the fully closed position and the Alaska's propeller stopped. Auxiliarymen securely tied the sub to the pier.

"Secure the Maneuvering Watch," the Chief of the Boat announced over the 1MC.

This is the moment submariners looked forward to more than any other. Only this time, they didn't have to wait until the end of a 70-day patrol. Almost the entire crew poured out of the sub and onto the pier to reunite with their loved ones after this short, strange trip.

Admiral Connery and the kids made their way through the crowd of sailors and families. Recognized by the crewmembers as the children of their lost shipmates, they were overwhelmed by hugs and words of condolence by this extended Navy family. When they crossed the gangplank onto the flat missile deck of the sub, they were greeted by the XO.

"Uncle Charley!" Caroline yelled out, as she embraced the Executive Officer.

"Caroline, this ship belonged to your father, and now I'm giving it to you," the XO whispered in her ear. "It's your job to make sure he gets it back."

The XO saluted the Admiral and then shook his hands to secretly pass a folded piece of paper he'd been hiding.

"Enjoy the tour of the sub," the XO said aloud so that everyone in the area could hear. "I've got a debriefing to attend so I won't be able to join you." With that, the XO crossed the gangplank and walked into the crowd of people on the pier.

The Petty Officer of the Watch gave a sharp salute to the famous retired Admiral and proceeded to assist the group through the hatch. The sub was a ghost town. Once everyone was safely below, they were greeted by the Chief of the Boat.

"Welcome aboard the Alaska, everyone," the Chief proclaimed. "The Skipper informed me that this tour might run a little longer than usual. Excuse me while I climb up and secure the hatch above you. We wouldn't want anyone to drop in unexpectedly."

The Chief slammed the missile deck hatch shut and spun the wheel to seal and lock it. Upon climbing back down, he picked up a sound-powered phone.

"Control, this is the Chief of the Boat," he spoke. "Secure all hatches."

"Secure all hatches, Control, Chief of the Boat, aye," a voice replied.

With that, hatches on the sub's hull and sail were closed and locked so that no one from the outside could enter the giant steel cylinder.

Annie jumped at the sound of the hatches slamming shut. "I feel trapped!"

"I'm feeling claustrophobic," Mike chimed-in.

"Admiral, the crew of the Alaska awaits your orders," the Chief announced, as he stood at attention before Admiral Connery.

"Thank you, Chief," replied the Admiral. "I wasn't actually sure how this was going to play out."

"You're among friends," the Chief of the Boat said to the Admiral and kids. "The XO hand-picked those of us who would remain aboard once we docked. We are loyal to him, and your dads are like brothers to us. While the officers and men on the pier would be sympathetic to your plight, they don't know anything about this and therefore have plausible deniability. I guess the XO wanted to make sure that only a few of us end up serving jail time in Leavenworth. Since I don't have a full section of men onboard, you kids will have to help out with some of the watch stations."

"I'm officially a junior Fire Control technician," Nick interrupted the Chief's speech. "I can plot solutions and fire torpedoes."

"Yeah, and Chrissie and I can drive this thing anywhere you want to go." Annie motioned her hands in the air like she was turning a steering wheel.

"The kids received training on diving and driving the ship this morning at TriTraFac, so they should be more of a help than a hindrance," the Admiral remarked.

"That's great news," the Chief replied. "We have a working nuclear reactor, a full complement of Mark 48 torpedoes, 24 Trident II D5 missiles, plenty of air and water, and enough food to last us a few weeks. Let's move forward to Control so we can get underway. It won't be long before somebody topside starts to get suspicious."

As the group moved forward through the passageways, Mike pulled out Wi-Fi access points from his backpack and plugged them in every so often in order to stitch together a wireless network for the kids.

"Are we really going to need this stuff?" Caroline asked as she watched Mike geek-out.

Upon reaching the Control room, the Admiral greeted the other crewmembers and then grabbed the 1MC microphone next to the periscope.

"Station the Maneuvering Watch," the Admiral ordered over the 1MC.

The children ran to the stations on which they'd trained earlier in the day and the Admiral sat in the Officer of the Deck's chair.

"Helm, ahead one-third," commanded the Admiral.

"Ahead one-third helm, aye," Annie replied, as she twisted the engine order telegraph to the 1/3 position with a ring of the bell.

Back in Maneuvering, a bell rang and an indicator displayed "Ahead 1/3." Luckily, the ship's engineer, the Eng as he's called, had decided to put his own naval career in jeopardy and was onboard so he could spin the large wheel one full rotation to the right. With that, the reactor's steam drove the turbine which caused the giant propeller at the back of the sub to rotate.

"Rudder amidships." The Admiral barked out his next order to Annie.

"What does that mean?" Annie asked frantically.

"It means steer us straight," replied Admiral Connery.

Topside on the pier, a Marine was tripped by a rope connected to the submarine as it moved forward along the dock. The large crowd of crewmembers and loved ones who hadn't gone home yet noticed this and began to ask each other if this was planned or not. Some started following the sub down the pier and a few others made phone calls to squadron personnel.

"We've got unauthorized movement of one of our submarines!" A Lieutenant yelled into his walkie-talkie as he walked briskly along the pier.

The Petty Officer of the Watch who had previously ushered the group of kids inside the sub had already begun running up and down the length of the 560-foot submarine when each of the hatches had slammed shut. He made calls to the ship's radio room but got no answer. When he saw the propeller spinning, his heightened sense of panic caused him to pull out his gun; he then sounded the alarm and called the Commander of Submarine Squadron 17.

"Admiral Cunningham, this is Petty Officer Jimenez," the Petty Officer said frantically through his headset. "The USS Alaska has been sealed shut and is underway westward along the Delta pier."

"Who's onboard the ship right now?" Admiral Cunningham asked.

"According to my log, we have a small skeleton crew, which isn't too unusual in the first moments after we arrive home," replied Petty Officer Jimenez. "We also had a pre-arranged tour of the sub for Admiral Connery and the group of kids whose fathers all died. They came through the missile deck hatch that I've been guarding."

"What about the other hatches that you haven't been guarding?" the Admiral pressed.

"There's been a lot of commotion since we docked at the pier so it's possible, but not likely, that someone could've entered through one of the other hatches," the Petty Officer replied timidly.

"You idiot!" The Admiral screamed into the phone. "For all I know, terrorists or agents of a foreign government could be stealing the Alaska right now with all those innocent children onboard. I don't need this. Phone down to the boat to make sure that this isn't a big misunderstanding before I call in the cavalry."

"I've tried, sir," responded Jimenez. "The sound-powered phone lines are cut and I get nothing but static when trying to contact the radio room. No one from the

Alaska has tried to contact me so I have no idea what's going on inside."

"I've heard enough," Admiral Cunningham barked through the phone. "I'm going to end this right now."

Fewer than thirty seconds passed before a squadron of Marines arrived on the scene in their Humvees and started firing machine guns at the submarine. Hearing the bullets hit the hull, the kids inside started to scream.

"They're going to kill us!" Mike shouted in the control room.

"Hold your fire!" One of the Naval Officers on the pier yelled out to the Marines. "There's still a Petty Officer topside on the missile deck and I don't think your bullets are going to make a dent in the HY-180 steel submarine hull either."

The giant vessel started to pull away from the pier. When the long ropes that kept the sub tied to the cleats became taut, it was unable to move any further. A loud, groaning sound echoed down the pier as the metal cleats began to bend. Onlookers started backing away from over-stretched ropes holding the Alaska in place.

"Helm, all-ahead flank," commanded the Admiral. "We need to break free of the pier."

"All-ahead flank, aye," Annie repeated.

Back in Maneuvering, the Eng turned the giant wheel until all the steam the reactor could make was pushing the turbine to spin the propeller faster than ever. The churning water sprayed everyone on the dock with icy-cold salt water.

After straining to the breaking point, all of the ropes snapped and the submarine broke free. The cleats holding the lines ripped from the pier and smashed into the Humvee, narrowly missing the heads of the Marines. With nothing holding it back now, the sub lunged forward and everyone inside fell over.

Petty Officer Jimenez found himself thrown from the top of the sub and into the water.

"Reduce your speed to ahead 1/3 and come right to heading 000," ordered the Admiral.

"Reducing my speed to ahead 1/3 and coming right to heading 000, aye," Annie replied nervously to the Admiral.

Back in the Squadron 17 building on the Delta pier, the Squadron Commander looked out the window at the chaos below and dropped his head into his hands. He watched people running frantically to get away from a sparking power cable that just snapped free from the departing sub.

"This can't be happening!" the Commander yelled out in his empty office. Noticing the phone on his desk, he quickly picked it up to call the tugboat that had previously guided the Alaska to the pier.

"This is Admiral Cunningham," the Squadron Commander announced through the phone. "I want you to tell your tug pilot to block the Alaska's path so it can't make it north up the Hood Canal."

"I'm not interested in putting my boat in that kind of danger Commander," replied the pilot. "I don't care what you're interested in!" the Commander shot back. "Block that sub or the only thing you'll be piloting is a rubber duck in your bathtub!"

The tugboat gunned its engines and set an intercept course for the Alaska.

Back on the Alaska, Admiral Connery was looking through the periscope and could see the approaching vessel.

"Helm, all-ahead full," he ordered. "I don't want that tug to crack our sonar dome."

The big ballistic missile sub came to life and raced ahead up the canal. By the time the two vessels intersected, the tug was no longer able to block the Alaska and crashed midway into its starboard hull. The sub shook violently but the tug got the bad end of the deal as it bounced off and started taking on water, its engines quickly flooded, forcing the tug out of action. With that, the Alaska made its way north towards its next obstacle, the Hood Canal Bridge.

Fulfilling their part of the mission, an SUV containing Mike's and Chrissie's moms headed northwest out of Poulsbo toward the Hood Canal Bridge at a high rate of speed.

"I hope we don't get pulled over by the cops," Chrissie's mom Ashley spoke frantically.

"Don't sweat the small stuff," replied Mike's mom Michelle. "Our husbands might be alive, our kids are heading into danger on a stolen submarine, and the Marines are shooting at them."

"Good point," Ashley commented. "I guess I just need to play it cool and act like we know what we're doing."

The Hood Canal Bridge was created by the military and serves as the only way for people living in the northern

Olympic Peninsula to cross North America's largest fjord. The bridge can only be opened by the Navy to allow submarines in and out of the Hood Canal, greatly inconveniencing motorists on either side who need to get across. It has a control tower near the center where naval personnel can open or close this submarine gateway.

Admiral Cunningham from Squadron 17 placed a phone call to the petty officer manning the bridge.

"Petty Officer, the USS Alaska has been hijacked by an unknown group of hostiles and is heading your way," Admiral Cunningham announced. "Under no circumstances are you to let that submarine through."

"Yes, sir, Admiral," the Petty Officer replied. "No one's getting through here today."

"One other thing." The Admiral paused. "Make sure that your sidearm is available, just in case. This situation is critical to our national security."

The SUV arrived at the bridge and Ashley and Michelle made their way into the tower. "I know you're scared," Michelle whispered. "Just act tough and let's do the SWAT team thing."

"Got it!" Ashley whispered back as she kicked open the door to the control room to let Michelle inside.

"Open the bridge right now or I'm taking you down!" Michelle pointed her son's airsoft gun menacingly at the Petty Officer. "Don't make me kill you."

"I'm afraid I won't be able to do that," the Petty Officer replied, turning around with his 45 drawn. "Conspiracy to steal a Trident submarine with 24 ICBMs is treason and punishable by death. I don't know which government you work for, but you won't get very far in this business using a gun with an orange muzzle on the tip."

Ashley was hiding just outside and called her daughter to let her know that they had failed in their mission to subdue the Petty Officer and get the bridge opened. Chrissie relayed the bad news to the Admiral and everyone else in the sub's control room.

"There's no going back," Admiral Connery proclaimed. "Chief of the Boat, do we have any Torpedomen down below?"

"Yes sir," replied the Chief of the Boat. "What in the world do we need torpedoes for?"

The Admiral picked up his sound-powered phone and twisted the dial to the torpedo room.

"Torpedo room, Conn, make torpedo tubes one, two, three and four ready in all respects," the Admiral ordered through the phone.

"Make torpedo tubes one, two, three, and four ready in all respects, Conn, Torpedo room, aye," replied the Torpedoman on the other end of the line.

Down in the torpedo room, the men began the process of getting the torpedoes ready to launch. Fortunately, torpedo tubes one, two and three were already loaded. Using a sophisticated block-and-tackle system, they lifted the fourth torpedo off its rack and carefully loaded it into the open tube. They quickly ran diagnostic tests on the tubes to verify they were ready to shoot.

"Conn, Torpedo room, tubes one, two, three and four are loaded and ready to go," the Torpedoman exclaimed.

"I'm not comfortable with arming torpedoes inside the Hood Canal sir."

"Do your job and keep your comments to yourself," replied the Admiral.

"Fire control, plot a firing solution to the bridge," the Admiral commanded. "This should be easy since the bridge is directly in front of us."

"Admiral, the bridge is full of people," replied Nick.

"Plot a firing solution or I'll find someone else to do it," the Admiral snapped back impatiently.

"Yes, sir," replied Nick. "Hey, is anyone in the sonar shack?" he yelled out down the passageway. "I need a ping to verify range to the Hood Canal Bridge."

Without a reply, the sound of a loud ping echoed through the control room. Ping! The digital readout on Nick's fire control panel went from zero to 1,500 yards. Using what he learned from his training class just hours before, Nick plotted a simple firing solution that would shoot the torpedo directly ahead with a range of 1,500 yards and closing.

"The firing solution is ready," Nick exclaimed.

"Torpedo room, Conn, open the outer door and flood torpedo tube one," Admiral Connery spoke.

"Opening the outer door and flooding torpedo tube one, aye," replied the Torpedoman. "You better know what you're doing, old man."

"You're relieved," the Admiral ordered.

"You're letting your missing son cloud your judgment, Admiral!" The Chief of the Boat got up in the Admiral's face.

"I know what I'm doing, COB," countered the Admiral.

"Chrissie, call your mom and tell her she has less than a minute to clear the bridge." The Admiral motioned.

Chrissie frantically dialed her phone.

"Mom, you've got to get everyone off the bridge right way!" Chrissie screamed into the phone. "We're going to blow up the bridge with one of our torpedoes. Hurry, get out of there!"

Ashley burst into the bridge control room to see the Petty Officer pointing his gun at Michelle.

"Looks like we have company," the Petty Officer remarked. "Let me guess, you probably brought a rubber knife to take me down, right?"

"Okay, I admit it, we're not commandos." Michelle held her hands up in the air.

Ashley turned to the Petty Officer. "Unfortunately, we have a little problem here. The thing is, if you don't open this bridge, the Alaska is going to blow it up with its torpedoes."

"You're bluffing," said the Petty Officer.

"I'm no Texas Hold'em player, but are you willing to bet your life on that?" she retorted. "Are you going to bet the lives of all these civilians in their cars on the bridge? We're all going to be dead in the next minute."

The Petty Officer turned to the window and his demeanor changed when he saw the approaching submarine. He immediately pulled down a lever that lowered crossing-guard arms on both ends of the bridge and then picked up a microphone.

"Ladies and gentleman," the Petty Officer spoke. "You have less than a minute to get out of your cars and run back to shore. Clear the bridge immediately. This is an emergency. Run!"

Complete hysteria ensued on both sides of the Hood Canal Bridge.

The Petty Officer looked back at Mike and Chrissie's moms. "I'll make sure all these civilians are safe, but my orders are clear; I will not let the Alaska and the enemies of America through this bridge."

Back on the Alaska, Admiral Connery ordered, "Nick, shoot torpedo one."

"What about the people on the bridge?" Nick pled with the Admiral.

"Just trust me," replied Admiral Connery.

Nick pushed the firing button for torpedo tube one. Seconds later, with the assistance of 1,500 PSI hydraulic power, a giant water-ram inside the tube forced the water and torpedo out of the sub. The Alaska shuddered and everyone felt a whoosh as it fired a torpedo out into the Hood Canal.

From the bridge tower, the Petty Officer looked on in disbelief as a giant bullet of water and bubbles emerged from the sub.

Michelle screamed, "We've got to get out of here!"

"Oh my God, they really did it!" yelled the Petty Officer. "Our only chance to survive is to open the bridge and hope the torpedo will pass through the opening."

"Hurry! Do it before we get blown to bits," Michelle shouted.

The Petty Officer turned his back on the sub and ran to the control panel. He hammered his fist on the large red button, opening the bridge.

Meanwhile, panicked people on the bridge ran for the shore, leaving their cars behind.

"There's a torpedo coming right at us!" screamed a woman, as she ran from her car carrying her baby.

On the Alaska, Admiral Connery looked through the periscope and could see the bridge begin to open.

"Helm, all-ahead flank, cavitate," commanded the Admiral. We've got to catch up to the torpedo and get through the open bridge before they change their minds.

Back in Maneuvering, the Eng spun the wheel as fast as he could to apply all of the power of the reactor's steam to the turbines.

"Admiral, the torpedo has made it to the bridge opening," Nick called out to Admiral Connery. "Do you want me to detonate it?"

"Negative," replied the Admiral. "Let the fish pass through the opening and then deactivate it. I want it on the bottom of the Hood Canal where it won't hurt anyone."

Back in the bridge control tower, the Petty Officer remained almost frozen in terror as he watched the torpedo pass through the bridge opening. Almost another minute passed before he snapped back to reality.

"We're still alive," exclaimed the relieved Petty Officer. "I wonder why they didn't blow us up?"

He got his answer when he heard Alaska's fog horn blow as it passed through the open bridge trailing 500 yards behind the torpedo. The Petty Officer spun around and pushed the button to close the bridge - but it was too late; the Alaska had made it past its last physical barrier.

Once the bridge reconnected, Marine Humvees made their way across to the tower. Moments later, the door busted open and Marines armed with M16s flooded the room.

"Both of you put your hands on your heads and get on your knees." A large Marine motioned to Michelle and Ashley. "Petty Officer, you're under arrest for disobeying a direct order. And you two," he said pointing the machine gun towards the women," you're under arrest for conspiracy to steal a submarine. We're well within our rights to shoot you both right here and now for committing treason. Take them away."

The Marines led the three of them out of the tower and into one of the Humvees at gunpoint.

Meanwhile, people who had been on the bridge and watched everything transpire began to open their cell phones and make calls. The situation was no longer contained - the Navy's secret was out!

The White House

"Mr. President, someone has stolen one of our submarines," the National Security Advisor said as he barged into the Oval Office. "A Trident, no less."

"NSA, take us to DEFCON three while we try to figure this out," responded the President. "Where is this happening? Kings Bay or Bangor?"

"Bangor, sir," the NSA replied.

"Put me in contact with whoever's in charge at the scene," ordered the President.

"I've got COMSUBRON 17 on the line for you right now." The NSA pointed to a flashing light on the President's desk phone. The Commander in Chief quickly picked up the phone.

"Admiral, how could something like this happen?" the President asked sternly.

"We don't know, sir," replied Admiral Cunningham. "Our information is still very sketchy at the moment."

"Well then, tell me what information you do have!" The President's voice grew impatient.

"Right after the Alaska returned home, it was hijacked while most of the crew was on the pier," stammered the Admiral.

"The Alaska?" the President said with a curious tone.

"Mr. President, retired Admiral Connery and the children of the deceased Alaska Captain and crewmembers went onboard the sub for a tour immediately after it docked," Admiral Cunningham continued.

"I just conducted a funeral service a few weeks ago over at Arlington for the Alaska's skipper and some of his crew," the President grumbled. "This seems like more than a coincidence. Are you saying that a bunch of kids just made off with the most powerful weapon in my arsenal?"

"I'm not saying that at all," replied the Admiral. "We can't get through to them via radio so we don't know what's going on inside or who's in charge. I'm worried that Admiral Connery and those kids just happened to be in the wrong place at the wrong time when this theft took place."

"I'm losing patience with you, Admiral!" The President yelled into the phone. "The sub doesn't drive by itself. We're facing the largest threat to national security since the Cuban missile crisis and you've basically got nothing for me. Please tell me you have the situation in hand and the submarine is contained in the canal."

"Actually, sir, the Alaska just made it through the Hood Canal Bridge," Admiral Cunningham's voice trembled.

"You're relieved of duty." The President slammed down the phone. "Get me the Joint Chiefs; I'm headed to the Situation   Room."

CHAPTER 5 > THE CHASE

Hood Canal, Washington

The Alaska made its way out of the Hood Canal and entered the Strait of Juan de Fuca. A large and deep body of water, this gave the submarine more room to maneuver.

"Helm, come left to bearing two-seven-zero," Admiral Connery ordered. "We're headed west to the Pacific to find my son and your dads."

"Coming left to bearing two-seven-zero, helm aye," replied Annie.

"Have we left all the trouble behind us, Granddad?" Caroline asked.

"Caroline, I have a feeling that most of our troubles lie ahead." The Admiral put his arms around his granddaughter. "Envisioning the completed mission, relying on your training, following a plan, and maintaining a positive mental attitude are the keys to success for a sailor."

"How do I envision a completed mission if I haven't completed it yet?" Mike asked. "Just close your eyes and see yourself with your father after you've rescued him," replied the Admiral. "Never let go of that vision."

Seattle, Washington

Word of what was happening on the Olympic Peninsula was spreading fast. Two news helicopters lifted off from the rooftops of towers in downtown Seattle and made their way across the Puget Sound.

The White House

"Mr. President, now that the Alaska has made it to the open waters of the Strait, I think our best option is to take it out before it can dive into the Pacific beyond our reach," said an Air Force General, as the other Joint Chiefs entered the room.

"General, don't you have even the slightest concern over the repercussions of blowing up a sub containing 24 ICBMs plus a nuclear reactor?" the Chairman of the Joint Chiefs asked. "At best, we could have an ecological nightmare that would make the BP oil spill in the Gulf look like spilled milk! At worst, we could have an atomic explosion in US waters."

"Mr. Chairman, I understand your concerns, but we've got to find a way to stop this thing," the President said urgently. "It's not moving very fast, but it's made of some amazingly tough steel and we can't get inside of it to take control."

"What if we used a low-yield, laser-guided bomb and targeted just the bow of the sub?" a four-star Admiral spoke-up.

"The sonar dome?" asked the President.

"That's right, Mr. President," the Admiral replied. "We could deploy a SEAL team in a combat rubber raiding craft that could paint the sonar dome with a laser. One of our fighter-bombers could target just that part of the sub, away from the reactor and the nukes."

"I'm listening." The President leaned forward across the table.

"The Alaska would slowly flood from the front and begin to sink nose-first," the Admiral continued. "The ICBMs wouldn't explode and the reactor wouldn't flood since it's protected by water-tight doors. Additionally, the reactor would scram and automatically drop the control rods once the downward pitch becomes too steep."

"The Strait of Juan de Fuca is a heck of a lot shallower than the Pacific Ocean," a Homeland Security official added. "We could dispatch ships, equipment and DSRVs to search for survivors and then raise the Alaska to the surface."

"I don't think it would come to that." The Chairman jumped in. "I'm sure the minute that boat starts taking on water, they'll cut their engines and escape hatches will start popping open. The SEALs on the scene could board the Alaska, take out the hostiles and secure enough watertight doors to stop the flooding."

"What if they don't pop the hatches?" the Marine Commandant queried.

"Then we'll do it the hard way and let the Alaska sink to the bottom," replied the Chairman. "Divers could come in later with underwater blow torches and cut their way through the hull."

"I'm sold," the President exclaimed. "It's not pretty, but we don't have a lot of time. Admiral, get SEALs in the water and launch the fighter-bombers from the Naval Air Station on Whidbey Island."

"Very good, sir," replied the Admiral.

Strait of Juan de Fuca

The news helicopters from the KING 5 and KOMO 4 television stations tracked the giant submarine from the air as it passed next to Dungeness Spit.

"Get cameras rolling," the producer yelled to the cameraman over the sound of the helicopter rotors. "I haven't seen a slow-motion chase like this since I followed O.J. down the San Diego freeway."

"No one got a Pulitzer Prize for covering O.J.," the cameraman called back.

"This is much bigger!" the producer shouted. "Big like when Captain Kirk stole the Enterprise to rescue Spock."

"Dude, your whole life is a movie," the cameraman replied with a laugh. "Position the satellite dish and let's start sending this home so our boss won't think we're on a wild goose chase."

Within minutes, the video of the fleeing submarine began streaming back to television stations in Seattle. Upon seeing what was going on, station managers interrupted their regularly scheduled programming with a breaking story and team coverage. The story quickly went viral and images of a submarine being chased by boats and helicopters were beamed to TVs, computer monitors, smartphones and iPads all around the world in vivid HD 1080p.

Poulsbo, Washington

Sitting at home watching the news, Caroline's mom saw the waterborne chase and immediately picked up her Windows Phone to text her daughter.

"CAROLINE, IT'S MOM. UR ON TV"

USS Alaska

"Hey everyone, we're on TV!" Caroline yelled throughout the control room after reading the text. "Helicopters are directly above us with video cameras. Is there a TV we can turn on around here?"

With that, a Yeoman began to run throughout the sub turning on every TV he could find. When Caroline changed the channels on the TV in the Control room, she saw the same images of their submarine that the rest of the world was seeing. The breaking news crawler inching across the bottom of the screen turned her blood cold.

"…U.S. SUBMARINE HIJACKED BY TERRORISTS…"

"But we're not terrorists," Caroline protested, as she looked at her grandfather.

"Obviously, neither the Navy nor the President believes we have anything to do with this," commented Admiral Connery. "If they think terrorists are behind this, I expect the military will come at us with everything they've got."

Naval Air Station, Whidbey Island

"You're all clear for takeoff," said a voice from the control tower.

"Roger that," replied the pilot.

With that, the F/A-18 Super Hornet ignited its afterburners and screamed down the runway, blue flames shooting out from its twin engine exhausts.

"I'm going supersonic and should arrive at the submarine's coordinates in ten minutes." The pilot spoke to the air boss in the control tower.

USS Alaska

As the Alaska continued its westerly course through the strait, many of the kids and crew couldn't help but watch the unfolding action on the TVs throughout the ship.

"I wish we could go faster," Mike sighed as he watched his sub on the overhead monitor.

71

"A Trident submarine isn't exactly a cigarette boat," Admiral Connery spoke, looking over at Mike. "She's designed to perform at her best underwater."

"I'm not sure what a cigarette has to do with a boat, but that small, black rubber boat on the TV sure is moving fast and looks like it's about to catch us," remarked Mike.

Admiral Connery peered into the periscope and rotated it to the starboard side. A speeding boat with several men onboard came into view.

"Good observation, Mike," the Admiral commented without looking away from the periscope. "That boat is a combat rubber raiding craft, so I can only assume that the men holding machine guns are SEALs. I wonder what they're up to?"

F/A-18 Super Hornet

"Patch me through to the SEALs on the water," the pilot ordered through his mask.

"Patching you through," replied the air boss.

"Special forces, do you read me?" asked the pilot.

"We read you," answered a Lieutenant on the speeding boat. "What is your ETA to our location?"

"I'll be in range in five minutes. Begin lasing the target now," the pilot ordered.

"Roger that," replied the SEAL Lieutenant. "We'll paint you a nice big target on the sonar dome for your precision ordinance."

"Make sure you're a safe distance away," the Pilot added. "I don't want to see any mention of friendly fire on my next fitness report."

"Nice," remarked the Lieutenant. "I'm turning the laser on now."

USS Alaska

"What's that red light beaming at us, Granddad?" Caroline asked as she watched the television.

Through the periscope, the Admiral could clearly see the SEALs painting a target on the bow of the sub.

"Change of plans everyone," Admiral Connery remarked intensely. "Those SEALs are targeting our sonar dome for a laser-guided bomb. That means we're just moments away from being attacked by incoming aircraft. We're no longer safe on the surface."

"Diving Officer, Emergency Deep!" The Admiral shouted to Caroline.

"Emergency Deep? We didn't learn about that in the trainer this morning!" Caroline panicked.

"It means dive the ship as fast as you can," barked the Admiral. "Mike, open the vents to let out the air and fill the tanks with seawater. Chrissie, I need you to push your yoke all the way down to give us a full downward angle on the stern planes. Annie, once the sail is submerged, I want full down on the fairwater planes, too."

The Admiral picked up his microphone and announced, "Dive, Dive, Dive," on the 1MC. He then sounded the klaxon, which made an annoying sound that the kids had only heard previously in movies.

A large spray of air and water shot up from the deck of the Alaska as she slowly began to slip beneath the waves.

"We're not sinking fast enough," the Admiral groaned.

SEAL Team

"They're submerging!" The SEAL Petty Officer holding the laser yelled out to the Lieutenant.

"Keep the sonar dome painted as long as you can," the Lieutenant ordered frantically.

The SEAL team could hear the thundering sound of incoming fighter jet as it approached their position.

"The bomb is going to be here any second now," the Lieutenant pronounced loudly. "Keep it painted."

"The sonar dome is almost completely under water," cried out the Petty Officer. "Call off the bomber."

"Too late," the Lieutenant replied, as the two of them heard the familiar whistling sound of the falling bomb.

The laser was no longer painting the sub but was instead pointing at the surface of the water. The reflection caused by the churning waves resulted in the laser-guided bomb making erratic course corrections as it fell through the atmosphere. These course corrections pushed it closer and closer to the boat the SEALs were on. Recognizing this, the SEAL Petty Officer switched off the laser and the bomb splashed harmlessly into the water about one hundred yards from their boat.

The F/A-18 Super Hornet dove towards the submerging Alaska and fired its 50 caliber guns angrily while the sail disappeared beneath the surface.

USS Alaska

The kids put their hands over their ears and screamed as the fighter jet strafed the Alaska from above. The impact of high-caliber bullets striking the hull of the sub sounded like the most terrifying hailstorm anyone could imagine. Fortunately, the bullets were harmless to the thick, double-hulled, Leviathan. In another minute, the sound of the attacking jet faded as the sub sank deeper into the strait.

"Diving Officer, make your depth two hundred feet," the Admiral ordered.

"Make my depth two hundred feet, aye," replied Caroline. "Can we really go that deep in here?"

"Some parts of the strait are nine hundred feet deep," responded the Admiral. "Our downward-facing, high-frequency sonar will let us know how much wiggle-room we have between the keel and the ocean floor."

In the sky above, the hovering news helicopters banked to the southeast and headed back to Seattle. Everything that had transpired was now streaming to the rest of the world. Underwater where it was less vulnerable, the submarine silently accelerated at flank speed away from the danger.

"I sure am glad we didn't steal a destroyer or some other surface ship," Annie said to the Admiral. "We'd be sitting ducks."

"You're going to make a great submariner," said Admiral Connery with a grin.

The White House

Back in the Situation Room, a messenger handed a piece of paper to the President.

"We've lost the sub." The President read the message out loud. "Damn it! How could this have happened?"

"There's more, sir." The messenger spoke quietly. "I've got the Russian President waiting to speak to you on a secure line."

The President put the phone to his ear. "Yes, Dmitry?"

"I've been watching the news on TV and I understand you've lost one of your ballistic missile submarines," the Russian President stated flatly. "Would you like our assistance in finding her?"

"It sounds to me like you've been watching 'The Hunt for Red October,' and not the news," the President retorted.

"The irony didn't escape me," replied the Russian President. "We would've tried much harder to sink the sub if it had been one of ours. And we wouldn't have allowed a spectacle like this to be captured and broadcast for all to see on television. We will have no choice but to put our military on high alert and raise our defense posture immediately."

"I assure you, we'll get her back," the President responded, hanging up the phone.

He turned to face the rest of the Joint Chiefs.

"This has gotten way too out of hand for half-measures anymore. I'm ordering you to dispatch the entire Pacific fleet, if necessary, to hunt down and sink the Alaska. A Trident submarine with enough firepower to destroy China has been stolen and has now left US waters."

"Take us to DEFCON One."

CHAPTER 6 > FINDING THEIR FATHERS

Defense Condition One represents the American military's highest level of alert, putting bombers in the air, getting troops ready to deploy, and preparing the land and sea-based nuclear arsenal for launch toward their target packages.

The United States has never found itself at DEFCON ONE...until now!

West coast naval stations in San Diego, Pearl Harbor, Everett, Bremerton, and Bangor received urgent messages to recall their sailors in preparation for heading out to sea to hunt down the rogue submarine.

USS Alaska

After an hour of running shallow at 200 feet, the Alaska finally left behind the Strait of Juan de Fuca and entered the

Pacific Ocean. At such a shallow depth and high rate of speed, US Naval forces would be able to track it with ease.

"It's time to turn this sub into a black hole in the water," Admiral Connery announced. "I'm sure every ship and sub within a thousand nautical miles has been contacted by the Commander of the Pacific Fleet and is now making best speed toward our location. Dive, make your depth 800 feet, zero bubble."

"Make my depth 800 feet, zero bubble, aye," replied Caroline. "Take her down nice and easy."

Annie pushed on the yoke ever so gently and the Trident began its smooth descent to 800 feet below the surface.

"Mind your planes," Caroline said curtly to Chrissie as the sub began to angle downward. "Keep us level."

"I got this," Chrissie snapped. "Stop telling me what to do!"

"I'm doing my job, Chrissie." Caroline walked around to face her. "You need to get used to this whole military chain of command thing if we want to succeed as a team. The Officer of the Deck tells me what to do and I tell you what to do. It's not personal."

Naval Undersea Warfare Center

The Marine Humvee carrying Mike's and Chrissie's moms arrived in Keyport, Washington, at the main gate of the Naval Undersea Warfare Center. After being waved through, the vehicle made its way to the base brig. Exiting the Humvee, Ashley and Michelle were led inside to a

79

makeshift interrogation room. The Marines forced them to sit down on two metal chairs and handcuffed them to the legs of a table that was bolted to the floor.

"Welcome to Torpedo Town, USA, ladies," sneered a dark-suited man, wearing dark sunglasses.

"You don't look like someone from the Navy." Michelle spoke up.

"That's okay, you don't look like terrorists or spies from a hostile government," the man retorted. "That doesn't mean you're not."

"Are you from the CIA?" asked Ashley.

"No, NCIS," the man replied. "Based on the sound of your voices, I can deduce that you were born and raised on American soil; that tells me you're part of a sleeper cell that's been operating in this country since at least the 1960s. Because that predates the Jihad against America, I can only assume that you're of the Cold War variety. I'm surprised you didn't return to Rodina back in the 90s."

"Rodina?" questioned Michelle. "What does a monster from Godzilla movies have to do with anything?"

"You're Russian spies." The NCIS agent snapped back at them, unamused.

"We're not Russians," Ashley protested. "We're Americans."

"Then why did you conspire to help the USS Alaska escape by taking control of the Hood Canal Bridge?" asked the agent.

"Listen, we're Navy wives." Michelle's voice became louder. "We're not conspirators and we want to see a lawyer."

"I'm afraid this isn't one of your TV crime dramas," the agent replied. "You've committed treason against the United States by aiding in the theft of one of our most powerful military weapons. No lawyers are coming and no one knows you're here. Now tell me who you work for and where that submarine is headed or things will become very uncomfortable for you."

"Our kids are on the Alaska." Ashley offered up this information quickly. "They're trying to rescue their fathers who disappeared in some kind of science and research vessel. We know our husbands are still alive out there. You're not going to torture us are you?"

The NCIS agent responded with a quizzical look on his face, "Do I look like Jack Bauer to you? Excuse me for a moment," he said, leaving the room to make a phone call.

USS Abraham Lincoln

The USS Abraham Lincoln and its battle group was returning to Everett, Washington, after spending nine months in the Indian Ocean in support of operations in Afghanistan. This massive aircraft carrier was designed to project power anywhere in the world with its 60 fighter jets and anti-submarine warfare planes and helicopters. The carrier's twin nuclear reactors reduced power to the turbines and the ship began to slow in response to an important flash traffic radio transmission.

Moments later, a Yeoman knocked nervously on the ship Captain's door.

"Come," replied the Rear Admiral.

"Admiral, I have an important message from COMPACFLEET," the Yeoman announced.

"What does Pearl want now?" the Rear Admiral uttered under his breath. "Don't they know we're almost home?"

The Yeoman handed the Admiral the message:

"TOP SECRET |COORDINATE BATTLE
GROUP AND LEAD EFFORTS TO SINK
ROGUE OHIO CLASS SUBMARINE | PROCEED
TO LATITUDE: 47.81 LONGITUDE: -126.71 |
SEAWOLF CLASS SUBS HEADING TO
COORDINATES TO ASSIST |
TARGET IS USS ALASKA AND IS ARMED
WITH TORPEDOES AND NUKES"

"Yeoman, I think your generation would say OMG when reading something like this," the Rear Admiral remarked. "I wonder what the significance of these coordinates is?" He then reached over and un-holstered a microphone from his stateroom wall. "Crew of USS Abraham Lincoln, man battle stations."

Battle stations alarms began to sound on every deck of the carrier, as sailors and aviators ran to their posts. Soon, the alarms spread to the Destroyers, Frigates, and Guided Missile Cruisers in the strike group. The curving wake behind all the ships meant that they were all changing course and heading for the mysterious GPS coordinates.

USS Alaska

"Annie, please maintain your depth of 800 feet," Caroline said as she watched the numbers on the depth gauge increase slightly.

"I don't know what's going on," Annie cried. "I've been pulling up on the planes but we're still losing depth."

"Granddad, there's something strange going on here." Caroline looked back at the Admiral. "We're beginning to sink."

"Helm, full rise on the fairwater planes," the Admiral barked.

"Full rise on the planes, helm, aye," Annie replied as she pulled all the way back on the yoke.

"Admiral, we're less than a mile away from the lat/long coordinates," Nick commented.

"We're driving ahead at flank speed, Annie's got her planes on full rise but we're still sinking." Caroline's voice took on a sense of panic.

"Mike, initiate an emergency blow and put us on the roof," the Admiral commanded sternly.

"Huh?" responded Mike with a blank look on his face.

"Reach up to the panel directly above your head and pull those two switches downward," the Admiral clarified. "Those are the chicken switches that will use high pressure air to blow the water out of the tanks and take us to the surface."

Mike reached up and pulled the switches. The sound of hissing echoed throughout the sub as the high pressure air pushed the water from the tanks and the Alaska began to rise.

"Chrissie, full rise on the stern planes," Caroline ordered.

With that, Chrissie pulled the outboard yoke all the way back and everyone could feel the bow of the sub angle upward. "I think this is doing the trick," said the Chief of the Boat, a grin beginning to appear on his face. "Hang on everyone; it's time for some serious angles." The Alaska quickly rose 100 feet. After rising another 50 feet, the sub's ascent began to slow and the kids started looking at each other with perplexed expressions.

"Is this normal?" inquired Mike.

"Not in the least." Admiral Connery looked worried. "We should be on the surface by now."

The Alaska eked out another 25 feet before it began to sink again.

"Admiral, not only are we sinking, but the ship's compass is going crazy and the inertial navigation system is behaving strangely." Nick exclaimed. "You know how you can make your hiking compass needle spin around if you hold a magnet up to it? It looks something like that."

At that moment, lights in the control room began to flicker, while the video monitors became distorted. A scared look came across everyone's faces as the Alaska wobbled and continued to sink with its bow pointed upward.

"All the extra air in the ballast tanks from the emergency blow is causing the boat to behave erratically as we sink," the Admiral exclaimed. "Mike, open the vents and refill the tanks with water and get us to zero bubble on the double.

Annie and Chrissie, zero your planes and work with Mike to get us level."

A chorus of "aye, sirs" came from the kids as they worked to stabilize the Alaska.

"I don't suppose there could be some kind of giant, super magnet out there that's causing our instruments to behave like this." Caroline thought out loud.

"Lucky for us, we're in a giant steel tube." Annie joked with the last ounce of humor in her body.

"Thanks for that, Annie," Mike retorted. "A giant magnet is actually the one thing that could explain both our sinking and why our navigation systems are freaking out. That's the smartest thing you've said all year, Caroline."

Caroline glared over at Mike without saying a word.

"So basically, there's some kind of magnetic force beneath us that's trying to pull us down to the bottom of the sea," Nick noted aloud. "Admiral, how long can we keep sinking before reaching crush depth?"

Without answering, the Admiral became lost in his thoughts for a moment.

"Torpedo room, flood torpedo tube two and prepare to fire on my mark," commanded the Admiral through his sound-powered phone.

"But, sir, I don't have a target solution to plug into fire control," said Nick from the fire control panel.

"I just want you to shoot the torpedo straight out of the tube at minimum velocity," the Admiral replied. "Open outer doors on torpedo tube two."

"Aye, aye, sir," replied Nick.

A moment later, the Admiral gave the order to shoot and a Mark 48 torpedo emerged from the open tube with a "whoosh." Everyone felt their ears pop as the air pressure changed inside the sub.

"Torpedo room, Conn, cut the wires," the Admiral ordered.

"But sir, how will we be able to steer the torpedo?" replied the Torpedoman.

"I don't want you to, and don't question my orders," the Admiral barked back.

"Conn, Sonar, I'm tracking the torpedo and it's beginning to lose depth control," the Sonarman announced.

"Sonar, Conn, aye," replied the Admiral. "That's what I was counting on."

The torpedo pointed downward and picked up speed as it headed toward the ocean floor.

"I want whatever magnetic force is out there to pull our metal torpedo right down to it," the Admiral explained. "I have a little surprise that it won't be expecting."

"Fire Control, arm the torpedo and set it to go active," commanded the Admiral.

"Sending HFIP command to arm torpedo and make it go active, aye," Nick replied.

The torpedo began pinging and, sure enough, it homed in on something that looked like a giant underwater radar dish pointing up from the ocean floor.

"I think the torpedo has acquired its target!" Nick yelled.

A second later the torpedo detonated a foot away from the dish, causing a giant underwater vacuum bubble that sent shockwaves in every direction.

The Alaska rocked backward and then sideways, knocking everyone off their feet as the shockwave hit. Cries and screams could be heard throughout the sub. A moment later, everything went dark and the propeller stopped spinning.

"My head is killing me." Caroline screamed out from the deck of the control room.

"Tell me about it," Mike echoed.

"I'm glad Annie and I were strapped into our seats," Chrissie exclaimed. "Click-it or ticket."

"Chief of Boat, we need emergency lighting," the Admiral ordered, slowly picking himself up off the deck.

"I'm on it, sir," replied the Chief.

A minute later, backup lighting flickered to life.

The Admiral picked up his sound-powered phone since it didn't need electricity to work. "All sections send in casualty and damage reports," he uttered into the receiver, as he dialed up every compartment on the sub.

One by one, reports came in from all over the sub. There were a number of bumps and bruises, but no serious damage to the ship. Then the report the Admiral most wanted came over his sound-powered phone.

"Conn, Maneuvering, the reactor's fine and I'm bringing propulsion back online," the Eng reported.

"That's music to my ears, Eng," replied the Admiral.

After what seemed like an eternity of silence, the welcome hum of the turbines was felt throughout the sub, bringing with it electricity and a spinning propeller to move the Alaska forward. Clapping and a little whistling could be heard by the delighted crew.

"Granddad, whatever was pulling us down before isn't doing it anymore." Caroline looked back at the Admiral.

"It appears that our torpedo did its job and took out that magnetic tractor beam," Admiral Connery said with a smile on his face.

"This is so awesome!" yelled out Mike. "We're on a real submarine and we just blew something up. This is better than the movies."

"No doubt," Nick echoed. "My friends are going to freak out when they hear we took out a tractor beam without the help of Obi-Wan Kenobi."

USS Seawolf

"Did you hear that?" a Sonarman asked the Chief next to him. "I've locked on an underwater explosion whose coordinates match the ones that we're heading to."

The Chief picked up the sound-powered phone.

"Conn, sonar, reporting an explosion at our target coordinates," the Chief announced.

"Sonar, Conn, aye," replied the Officer of the Deck.

"Chief of the Watch, float the buoy," the Officer of the Deck ordered. "We have an important transmission to make."

"Float the buoy, aye," replied the Chief of the Watch.

"Radio, Conn, when the buoy is at transmit depth, contact the Abraham Lincoln and tell them we have a submerged explosion at the same coordinates as our target destination," the Officer of the Deck said. "Tell them to have the battle group make their best speed to this location.

Something's going on down there and there's no time to waste."

The White House

"Mr. President, I just received a message from Pearl saying that SOSUS nets and sonars from multiple Pacific fleet submarines have detected a significant underwater explosion at the same coordinates as the original unidentified heat anomaly," the NSA announced. "The last known track of the USS Alaska, plus the NCIS confession report from the Hood Canal Bridge co-conspirators, leads us to believe that the sub was headed to the same location. The Abraham Lincoln battle group is en route to the coordinates as we speak."

"First a cruise ship, then the Omaha Beach and now the Alaska." The President sounded exasperated. "I met those so-called co-conspirators at a staged funeral for their husbands in Arlington. Things are starting to unravel around us."

Ocean Floor

The explosion rocked the Underworlder's crystalline structure. In the containment cell near the tip of the pyramid, the immobilized submarine sailors felt the same underwater shockwave that had tossed their children around in the Alaska.

"I wonder if someone's trying to fight for us?" Lieutenant Wyatt thought to himself.

USS Alaska

"Sonar, how deep is the ocean here?" asked Admiral Connery.

"Pretty shallow, just a thousand feet, sir," the Sonarman replied after taking a sounding.

"Use the downward scanning sonar to give me a map of the ocean floor and let me know if you detect anything unusual," Admiral Connery added.

The Alaska stopped moving and used its hovering computer to stay directly over the scene of the explosion.

"Admiral, in addition to pieces of wreckage from the explosion, I'm also picking up the cruise ship and a strange shape on the ocean floor," the Sonarman announced.

"What is it?" asked the Admiral.

"It looks like some kind of three-dimensional triangle jutting out from the seabed, sir," the Sonarman replied.

"Like a pyramid?" Admiral Connery asked.

"Yeah, how'd you know?"

The Admiral reached into his pocket and pulled out a piece of paper. The XO had written the word Pyramid on it. "Somebody you know gave me a heads-up," replied the Admiral.

"I'm also picking up a small cylindrical shape next to it," the Sonarman added. "It looks to be the same size as a DSRV."

"The Omaha Beach," the Admiral uttered under his breath. "We need to head down there and take a closer look."

"Chief of the Watch, work with sonar and set the hovering computer to take us down to 10 feet above the ocean floor," ordered the Admiral.

"Aye aye, sir," replied Mike.

"Okay team, here's the situation," the Admiral announced to everyone. "We've arrived at our destination and have identified the sunken cruise ship, a strange pyramid, and what looks to be the Omaha Beach. We're here to rescue your fathers and my son and therefore we need to get up close and personal with the DSRV sitting on the ocean floor."

"You mean go outside?" Chrissie asked.

"Exactly," responded the Admiral. "Chief of the Boat, how many of your crewmembers are qualified scuba divers?"

"None aboard, sir," replied the COB. "The two swimmers assigned to this boat went topside on the pier when the Alaska arrived in port."

"Well, can you spare any of your other crewmembers?" The Admiral sounded annoyed.

"Sir, we're running this sub with less than a skeleton crew. I can't even safely man each of the watch stations with what I've got."

"COB, we've come a long way and risked everything, not to be able to finish the job," the Admiral snapped angrily.

"I can do it," Caroline spoke up.

"Granddaughter, I appreciate you bravery, but you don't know the first thing about deep sea diving."

"I've got straight A's in school, so I bet I can figure it out if you'll show me what to do," Caroline answered. "You guys have a different manual to read for everything on this sub. Just give me the book with the procedure inside to perform this task and I'll make it happen."

"I'm sure you could figure it out." The Admiral nodded his head. "Your mother would kill me if I sent you out alone. It's just too dangerous to do this by yourself."

"She won't have to." Nick turned around from the fire control panel. "I'm going with her."

The Admiral sat silently for a few moments pondering the situation before him. "Alright, this is going to be the most reckless order I've ever given. Caroline and Nick, go get your deep-sea diving gear ready and report to the forward escape trunk. Go help them, COB."

"I guess we're going swimming in the deep end of the pool," Caroline said with a smile, as she fist-pumped Nick.

CHAPTER 7 > THE RESCUE

After Nick and Caroline suited up in their deep-sea diving gear, they climbed into the escape trunk. With Mike at his side, the Chief of the Boat closed the hatch behind them and sealed it shut. Flipping a switch enabled him to talk to Caroline and Nick from outside the compartment. "Alright kids, this is going to seem pretty weird." The Chief quickly spun a wheel allowing water to come flooding into the escape trunk. "I know it seems like I'm trying to drown you, but that's how this contraption works. I'm going to slowly fill the room you're in with seawater. Since you're wearing deep-sea diving suits, you won't have to worry about the pressure like you would if you were scuba diving. When the trunk is full and the pressure inside matches the pressure outside, the escape hatch will open."

"Roger that," Caroline responded.

A few minutes later, the escape hatch released, and Nick and Caroline left the sub. The weight of their suits prevented them from doing any actual swimming.

"Okay, this feels really weird." Caroline talked to Nick via their inter-suit communications system. "I know we're pretty far down, but I didn't realize the water would be so dark. We better switch on the coal miner lights in our helmets."

They walked along the missile deck on top of the Alaska and then jumped off the side to begin their descent to the ocean floor.

"That's one small step for man, one giant leap for mankind." Nick quoted Neil Armstrong as he landed on the sandy seabed.

"Don't forget about us girls," Caroline remarked.

"Sorry."

"Wow, forget what I said about the darkness. The bottom of the ocean seems to be glowing." Caroline motioned over to a mass of bio-fluorescent coral.

"I'm seeing millions of tiny glowing dots in the water." Nick waved his arms around.

"Hey! I see the Omaha Beach over there." Caroline pointed towards the DSRV as she walked softly across the seabed.

"Whoa, what's the giant pyramid thing behind the DSRV?" Nick asked.

"I don't know, but it looks like there's some kind of tube connecting the DSRV's forward escape hatch to the pyramid," Caroline remarked. "The tube looks transparent with a red glow inside."

"That crystal pyramid looks transparent too, but I can't quite see inside it," Nick added. "Weird. Anyway, I guess we need to find a way to enter the Omaha Beach."

The two kids proceeded across the ocean floor, climbed on top of the DSRV, and searched the outer hull looking for a way in.

"Hey, this looks like the same kind of hatch we just exited from on the Alaska." Caroline looked down at the metal steering wheel on the hull.

As the two of them knelt down to turn the wheel, they noticed a shadow pass over them.

"Oh my God Nick, it's a shark!" Caroline screamed as she watched the man-eater swim off into the distance.

Caroline and Nick put all their strength into turning the stubborn wheel. It wouldn't budge at first, but then it slowly started to move.

Nick looked up and noticed the shark circling back toward them. "It's coming back! We've got to try harder!"

Normally, the pressure of the seawater, combined with an empty escape trunk, would make it next to impossible to open the hatch. The Omaha Beach came equipped with hydraulically assisted arms that helped Caroline and Nick open the lid as water came rushing in to fill the empty room below. The two of them were caught off guard and sucked in with the rest of the seawater.

Dazed and disoriented, Nick stood up in the flooded escape truck and reached for the upper hatch to seal it shut. He recoiled in terror as the giant teeth, jaws and head of the shark came at him through the opening of the hatch.

"Get on the deck!" Caroline screamed as she pulled Nick downward to the floor of the escape trunk.

The shark was too large to fit through the escape hatch, but gnashed its teeth at them and violently whipped its head from side to side.

"I don't want to be eaten alive," Caroline cried.

"I think he's stuck." Nick pointed upward. "He can't get in past his fins, and he's completely sealed the hatch opening. It doesn't look like he can get out either. I guess they didn't teach him how to go in reverse at shark driving school." Nick managed some humor realizing that the immediate danger had passed. "We need to get the water drained out of here."

Looking across the room, Caroline noticed a clearly marked green button on the wall, and pushed it to force all the water out of the compartment. Once the escape trunk was empty, the shark began to suffocate since its gills were no longer moving through the water. The kids quickly took off their diving helmets and descended into the DSRV. Caroline took one last look at the dying monster above her and then sealed the lower hatch shut.

"The lights are on and everything seems to be working," reported Nick. "Maybe the power came back on after we torpedoed the tractor beam."

The two of them searched every compartment in the Omaha Beach but found no one around. They finally plopped down on a couple of seats that faced various control panels. Nick looked up at the giant display screen which gave him a view of the undersea world, including the USS Alaska. Caroline was staring at something more ominous.

"Hey Nick, look at that control panel above the weapons console." Caroline pointed above her head. "Do you see those two keys inserted in the panel?"

"OMG, I think those keys are inserted into the self-destruct system," Nick exclaimed. "They've both been turned to the right and the protective cover over the self-destruct button is open."

The two of them sat in silence for a moment as the gravity of what they had just seen sank in.

"I'm calling Granddad." Caroline walked over to the communications station. "I hope this fancy phone works." She placed the headset on her head and turned to the communications display. As luck would have it, the USS Alaska was listed as the last call placed, so she tapped on the screen and selected 256-bit encryption to make the call secure. A fake dialing sound helped Caroline pass the time while the connection was made to the Alaska.

"Silverdale Pizza, may I take your order?" Admiral Connery answered.

"I'd like a large Dyes Inlet special," replied Caroline.

"Nice to hear from you, granddaughter," the Admiral said with a smile on his face. "I'm glad you remembered our secret code. The Radioman didn't want to break radio silence but I was certain that the connection was coming from a nearby source."

"Granddad, Nick and I are on the Omaha Beach and the place is deserted," Caroline said. "Worst of all, we discovered that Dad and the crew tried to blow up their DSRV, after all. The self-destruct mechanism failed for some reason. But the self-destruct keys are still in!"

"It probably failed for the same reason all our electronics went haywire before we blew up that magnetic tractor beam," responded the Admiral. "Caroline, I need you to turn both of the keys counter-clockwise and pull them out. Keep one key in your pocket and give the other one to Nick."

"I'm doing it now, Granddad." Caroline turned the two keys and removed them from the panel.

"Where do you think everyone went?" Admiral Connery asked.

"I'm not sure, but the forward escape hatch is open with some kind of umbilical tube sealed over it," replied Caroline. "It looks like the tube leads to that large crystal pyramid structure that we saw sticking out of the seabed. Oh, one other thing. There's a red light shining from the hatch."

"I suppose if your dad and the rest of the crew aren't on the DSRV, then they must have left through the forward hatch and into the tube you're talking about," the Admiral said. "I'm sure they didn't leave the Omaha Beach willingly. They were probably taken, which means you could be next. I want you to get out of there and return to the Alaska immediately."

"Granddad, we've come too far to give up now." Caroline felt exasperated.

"Don't worry," the Admiral replied. "When you get back, I'll send some armed Alaska crewmembers to investigate."

"My Dad could be in danger right now," Caroline exclaimed. "I think Nick and I should go find him and the others."

"Under no circumstances are you allowed to enter that tube, young lady," barked the Admiral. "That's an order. Now get back to the Alaska."

"We can't go back now," Nick whispered to Caroline.

Caroline nodded, and then spoke into her headset.

"What was your last transmission?" Caroline asked. "Bzzzzz. There's some kind of interference and you're voice is breaking up. Crack, Bzzzz"

"I said get back to the Alaska this instant," repeated the Admiral.

Caroline placed the headset on the counter in front of her and motioned to Nick to get going.

"I totally dissed Granddad," Caroline said sheepishly. "We need to make our way through that tube and find our dads."

"Do you think it's safe?" Nick asked.

"Granddad doesn't seem to think so," replied Caroline. "I've got my Swiss Army knife, but let's try to find a gun or something."

"I don't see any weapons lying around, but there are a couple of those heavy Maglite flashlights mounted to the bulkhead," Nick said. "I've seen cops carrying those around."

"I guess we could always whack someone pretty good with one of those." Caroline smiled. "Hey, here's a rescue kit with a flare gun and a bunch of extra flares inside."

"That'll have to do," Nick commented. "Bring 'em." Nick handed Caroline one of the flashlights and they both climbed up the ladder through the forward hatch and into the tube. Once inside, they were bathed in an eerie red light. As they walked, they could see the ocean around them through the transparent walls.

"I wonder why they use red lights instead of natural or fluorescent light?" Nick asked.

"No telling," Caroline replied. "Look ahead to the end of the tube. It looks like there's a door to get into the crystal pyramid." When she reached out to turn the door handle, a blue bolt of electricity arced from the handle to her hand, causing her to fly backwards through the tube with a shock.

"Caroline!" Nick screamed as he ran over to her motionless body on the floor of the tube. "Oh, please be alive. Please start breathing."

Using the CPR training he learned in middle school, Nick started chest compressions as fast as he could. "Wake up, wake up, wake up!" Nick repeated with every compression.

After twenty seconds of furious effort, Caroline's eyes opened and she slowly sat up gasping for air. "I'm having trouble breathing," she said, between erratic inhales and exhales. "I think I just got struck by lightning."

"You got electrocuted by the door handle," said Nick. "I don't think we're going to get through that door with our bare hands. Got any ideas?"

"Gimme a sec," Caroline replied. "I'm just getting over not being dead. I feel really strange and I'm seeing all kinds of unfamiliar images in my mind. We obviously need to open the door with something that doesn't conduct electricity."

"Like a piece of wood?" Nick asked.

"I doubt we'll find any wood on the Omaha Beach," said Caroline.

As Nick turned away from her, Caroline noticed the rubber hose dangling from the air tank of his deep sea diving suit.

"Hey Nick," Caroline piped-up. "Since we're not swimming through the ocean and you're not breathing through your regulator, why don't we rip off your rubber hose and use it to turn the handle on the door?"

"Good idea," Nick replied. "That should keep us from being electrocuted."

Caroline reached over and unscrewed the hose from Nick's air tank.

"You get to open the door this time." Caroline smirked. "What could possibly go wrong?"

Nick wrapped the rubber tubing several times around his hand and proceeded to walk back to the pyramid door.

"Turn the handle to the left and then push it in toward the door," said Caroline.

"How do you know?" Nick replied.

"Don't ask me how I know." Caroline pointed at the handle. "I just know."

Reaching out with his rubber-wrapped hand, he grasped the electrified handle, turned it to the left and pushed. The door made an electronic buzzing sound followed by a metallic clank as the locking bolt retracted. With that, the door swung open inside the pyramid. The kids flipped on their flashlights and walked in.

No sooner had they entered the pyramid, an Underworlder lunged at Nick from behind the open door. He dropped his flashlight and they both fell to the ground. Nick felt a tremendous amount of heat through his heavy deep-sea diving suit in the places where the Underworlder's burning hands touched him. Nick began punching the creature in the face and kicked it in the gut with his knee.

"What are you?" Nick yelled out at the hairless creature, gazing into its ultraviolet eyes.

"Only your worst nightmare," the Underworlder snarled. "You and the rest of your filthy Overworlder species will soon vanish from the Earth."

Caroline immediately ran over to help Nick, but was repelled by a beam of intense heat, as the Underworlder pointed his hand in her direction, sending her flying across the corridor. The creature then turned his attention away from the sunburned girl and back to Nick.

"I'm finished with you Overworlder." The strange humanoid hovered over Nick. "For your sake, I hope you can hold your breath for a very long time."

Looking down at him, the Underworlder opened his mouth and a gauze-like substance extended from out of his throat and started wrapping itself around Nick's neck.

Nick looked up in horror as the gauze coming out of the Underworlder's mouth continued to wrap around his head covering his mouth and nose. "I can't believe I'm going to die this way," he thought to himself.

"Help me!" Nick yelled out through the last opening in the gauze.

"I'm coming!" Caroline responded weakly as she slowly lifted herself from the floor.

Just when things faded to black as the gauze covered Nick's eyes; the flashlight rolling on the floor shone its beam of light on the creature trying to mummify him. The Underworlder shrieked in pain as the rays of light made contact with his translucent skin. Wherever the light touched, smoke arose from its charred membrane. The Underworlder stopped wrapping Nick's head and reached for the flashlight. A weary but alert Caroline picked it up and trained the blinding light at the monster's face. Unable to endure the pain, the Underworlder gave up the fight and quickly disappeared down the glowing red corridor.

Caroline stumbled over to Nick and began cutting off the gauze with her Swiss Army knife. He inhaled deeply as she cleared his mouth and nose of the obstruction.

"Are you all right?" Caroline ripped the remaining gauze from his head.

"I think so," Nick replied.

"There are burn marks all over your suit and that stream of white cloth coming out of his mouth was creepy," said Caroline. "It reminded me of the Smoker Zombie from the Left 4 Dead video game. I swear it looked like he was turning you into a mummy."

"I guess it's a good thing I'm wearing this thick deep sea diving suit instead of a t-shirt and shorts," Nick said between coughs. "Remind me to bring a snorkel the next time some kind of freaky creature tries to mummify my head. Did you see the way he took off running and screaming when the flashlight shined on him?"

"I guess that answers your question about the red lights," Caroline said, looking at the red lights above her. "Whatever they are, they must not like our kind of light."

"Yeah, I suppose this infrared stuff is the only thing they can tolerate," responded Nick. "Did you check out those creepy glowing eyes?"

Caroline switched on her flashlight and handed Nick's to him as he got up off the floor.

"I guess it's a good thing we brought our low-tech light sabers," Caroline said with a smile. "I bet these creatures didn't know they were going up against a couple of Jedi warriors."

"You seem pretty okay considering we're inside an underwater pyramid and I just got attacked by a life form unknown to mankind with glowing eyes, burning hands and the ability to turn people into mummies," Nick commented.

"I've never been so scared in my life," admitted Caroline.

"What now?" Nick asked.

"Our fathers are being held in a room down this hallway." Caroline pointed. "And don't ask me how I know."

The two walked down the corridor, shining their flashlights in every direction to create a protective perimeter around them. After a few minutes of slow-motion walking, they came upon a translucent wall. Behind the glass lay a horrific sight.

Five mummified bodies were suspended by thin wires from the ceiling. They were held in a horizontal position with clear tubes coming up from their mouths.

"Caroline, those look like Egyptian mummies," Nick spoke quietly. "I wonder who they are?"

Looking beneath one of the mummies, Caroline noticed the gold submariner dolphin pin worn by her father lying on the floor. "Dad!" Caroline pounded on the glass.

"Look, Caroline!" Nick shouted. "I can see their bodies moving under the gauze. They're alive! How do we get in there?"

"There's a control panel on the wall over there," Caroline pointed at the panel. "I'm going to start pushing buttons until something happens." She ran over to the panel and tapped on different parts of the screen searching for the right button. Unfortunately, tapping on all those buttons set off the intruder alarm. "No, no, no!" she screamed. Undeterred, she closed her eyes, tapped the particular a sequence of buttons she saw in here mind and the glass wall disappeared.

The two of them ran to their dads and Caroline began cutting away the gauze with her knife. The sound of Underworlders running toward them could be heard in the distance.

"I think we've got company!" Nick looked down the corridor at dozens of glowing eyes heading their way.

"Nick, try to hold them off with the flare gun while I cut the gauze off our dads!" Caroline shouted. "Just buy me some time."

"Will do," replied Nick.

105

Caroline returned to cutting away gauze while Nick took out the flare gun and filled his pockets with extra shells. Leaving the containment room, he ran down the corridor toward the oncoming Underworlders.

"It's time for you to come into the light," Nick yelled at the hoard of Underworlders. He fired the flare gun directly at them, sending a blinding ball of burning light. The fireball landed on the floor just in front of them, causing the Underworlders at the head of the pack to squeal and shriek in anguish. Not only did the light burn their skin, but Nick noticed that their ultraviolet eyes turned black and the fleeing creatures seemed to bump into walls and each other during their retreat.

"Caroline," Nick yelled back over his shoulder, "I think the light blinds them as well. The Underworlders closest to the light are all crashing into each other as they try to get away."

"Awesome," Caroline replied. "I'm sensing their confusion."

She continued to cut the gauze off of Petty Officer Timbers, after freeing Petty Officers Love and Grant.

"I'm drained," commented Petty Officer Love, as he crawled slowly on the ground.

"Me, too," echoed Petty Officer Grant. "I've got nothing in the tank."

"Just do the best you can. Crawl down that hall toward the open door which will lead you out of the pyramid," Caroline told the freed crewmembers. "I'm almost done with Mike's dad."

Meanwhile, Nick had a grim look on his face as the light from the first flare died out. A second surge of Underworlders was approaching. Nick reached into his pocket to load another shell into his flare gun when an intense wave of heat forced him to drop the gun on the deck.

"Ahhhhh!" Nick screamed in pain as he was enveloped in burning heat. One of the approaching Underworlders sent a blast of heat from her outstretched hand. Once she lowered her hand, the heat disappeared.

Nick quickly reached down to pick up the gun, but a stream of white gauze shot at him and wrapped around his wrist. He looked up to see multiple streams of gauze coming at him from the open mouths of the oncoming Underworlders. The gauze wrapped around each of his arms and legs and lifted him up in the air. The creatures halted their approach and began reeling him in.

"Caroline, they've got me," Nick called out as he struggled in mid-air.

Caroline had just freed Petty Officer Timbers and sent him on his way toward the pyramid exit.

"I'm coming, Nick," she yelled, leaving her mummified father and Lieutenant Wyatt behind. In her haste to grab Nick, she accidently stepped on the flare gun and slipped to the ground. Seeing a flare shell on the deck, she quickly grasped it and loaded it into the gun next to her. She rose to her knees and pointed the gun toward the Underworlders. Closing her eyes, she squeezed the trigger launching a fireball between Nick and the creatures.

The burning flare sliced through the multiple streams of gauze and Nick crashed to the ground. The gauze connected to the Underworlders caught fire and the flames quickly moved toward the creatures who had tried to capture Nick. They shrieked with fright as the fire raced up into their open mouths.

Caroline and Nick winced as the Underworlders' heads smoldered and then turned to ash. The other Underworlders quickly backed off as they watched their comrades die before them. Nick handed Caroline the rest of the flare shells from his pockets and she repeatedly reloaded and fired the flare gun toward their new enemy. The fireballs and subsequent explosions looked like the grand finale from a Fourth of July fireworks show. The blinded and charred Underworlders were now in full retreat.

"The Underworlders are on the run, but I don't think it will be long before reinforcements return," said Nick.

"I agree," Caroline replied. "The other crewmembers should be out of the pyramid by now, so let's just drag our dads back to the Omaha Beach and get out of here."

With that, they cut down their fathers from the wires and began to drag them through the corridor toward the exit. It was slow-going, getting Captain Connery and Lieutenant Wyatt through the umbilical tube and down the hatch into the DSRV. Caroline made quick work of cutting off their gauze cocoons once inside the sub.

"We honestly didn't expect to see you guys again," Nick's father exclaimed. His eyes began to tear up.

"It's not just us, we brought the USS Alaska," replied Nick as he hugged his father tightly.

"You came for me." Captain Connery reached out and touched his daughter's face. "I love you, Dad." Caroline smiled at her father. "Of course I came for you. I'm a Connery. Uncle Charley risked his career and sent me a message telling me where you are."

"I'm sure the XO didn't intend for you kids to come rescue us," Captain Connery commented. "I would've expected SEALs."

"Commander Keller isn't onboard," Caroline said. "We brought Granddad, um, I mean Admiral Connery and all the rest of your kids. We kind of stole the Alaska. Those SEALs you were expecting to save you tried to kill us with a laser-guided bomb. To make matters worse, last we heard on the radio, the entire Pacific fleet is after us."

"You dragged my dad out of retirement for a suicide mission to come rescue us from these Underworlders?" Captain Connery looked incredulous.

"Actually, it was the Admiral's idea," replied Nick. "He needed a crew, so that's why we came along to help out."

"Like I said," Caroline raised her voice, "The entire Pacific fleet is on our tail, so we really need to get out of here."

"Hey, the lights are back on," Petty Officer Timbers remarked. "Some kind of tractor beam pulled us down here and disrupted our electrical systems."

"Yeah, but that disruption kept us from blowing ourselves up," added Petty Officer Love.

"No worries, we blew up their magnetic beam with one of Alaska's Mark 48 torpedoes," Admiral Connery proudly proclaimed as he emerged from the shadows.

"Granddad, what are you doing here?" a surprised Caroline yelled out.

"I figured you might need an extra deck hand," replied Admiral Connery. "Of course, I had to muscle my way past a shark to get here, but that just makes for a better sea story. It's time we get these engines fired up and close the forward hatch."

"Firing up the engines now," the Lieutenant Wyatt responded.

A weary Captain Connery stumbled over to embrace his father. "Thanks for not giving up on us, Dad," he whispered to the Admiral.

"It was your kids who didn't give up on you." Admiral Connery looked into the Captain's eyes. "They just needed an old bubblehead to teach 'em things like how to drive a submarine, take risks, shoot first, and ask questions later. As it turns out, risk-taking already seems to be in their DNA."

Meanwhile, Petty Officer Grant popped his head up through the forward hatch to see if the coast was still clear. It wasn't. Three Underworlders were running straight for him through the red glowing tube.

"We've got company!" Petty Officer Grant shouted to the crew below.

One of the Underworlders pointed his hand in Grant's direction; the Petty Officer felt a wave of intense heat come over him, causing him to fall down through the hatch.

"Gotcha," Petty Officer Love said, catching his falling shipmate.

The Underworlder chasing Grant wasted no time in diving through the hatch in close pursuit. The creature crashed onto the deck of the control room and began shrieking and writhing in pain in the fluorescent light-filled compartment.

"I guess nobody told this freak that the Omaha Beach got its power back." Nick backed away from the Underworlder who was flipping around the deck like someone having a seizure. "FYI, Caroline and I found out that these creatures can't stand our kind of light. Oh gross, it looks like its skin is sizzling."

The crewmembers covered the shrieking Underworlder in dark blankets and locked him in the one of the staterooms.

Admiral Connery grabbed his sidearm and raced up the ladder, out through the hatch and into the glowing red tube. An Underworlder tackled him and the two struggled on the floor of the tube. The Admiral was protected from the heat of the creature's hands since he was still wearing his deep-sea diving suit. He reached over and struck the Underworlder on the head with his gun and managed to break free. Admiral Connery crawled towards the hatch and stuck his head down through the opening.

"Get this sub moving," the Admiral shouted. "I'll hold off these monsters so you can get away!"

"Noooooo!" screamed Caroline. "We're not leaving you!"

She rushed up toward the open hatch and was immediately restrained by other members of the crew. She punched Petty Officer Timbers, knocking him to the deck. Finally, her father grabbed her and pulled the young warrior down the ladder as she kicked and screamed wildly.

"You heard the Admiral," exclaimed the Lieutenant Wyatt. "Let's get out of here!"

With that, Admiral Connery slammed the hatch shut from the outside and turned around to face the two remaining Underworlders. He lunged toward them, firing a fatal shot at one of the creatures. As the Underworlder fell to the floor of the tube, the Admiral pointed the gun at his other foe. The lone Underworlder quickly opened his mouth and fired a stream of gauze that wrapped around the Admiral's gun and yanked it out of his hand. Without missing a beat, the Admiral punched the Underworlder in the head, sending the humanoid falling to the floor. The Admiral quickly jumped on him trying to finish the fight. At that moment, he began to feel searing heat coming from the Underworlder's hands as it reached up and grasped his throat. Just as the heat became too unbearable to take, they both found themselves enveloped by the icy waters of the deep ocean as water rushed into the tube.

The Underworlders' umbilical tube ruptured as the DSRV's turbines came to full speed, allowing the Omaha Beach to make its escape upward from the ocean floor. From the giant display screen inside, everyone could see the ongoing underwater battle between the Admiral and Underworlder behind them. A shroud of bubbles began to encase the combatants as the creature's burning hands caused the water around them to boil.

"We can't leave Granddad!" Caroline cried uncontrollably as the image of the fearless Admiral became smaller and smaller. "Goodbye."

CHAPTER 8 > THE ESCAPE

The ocean floor trembled violently as the crystalline pyramid rose out of the sea bottom. Within minutes, the pyramid had completely dislodged itself from the sand and started to move slowly through the water. It became apparent that the structure only looked like a pyramid when buried underground with its tip exposed above the ocean floor. In fact, this vessel looked more like a giant diamond the length of a football field. An unknown energy source emanating from the Underworlder craft generated so much heat that the seawater around it boiled uncontrollably.

"Are you guys seeing what I'm seeing?" Nick asked everyone in the control room, as he stared at the diamond-shaped craft coming toward them. "Petty Officer Grant, I think we need to get the Alaska on the phone right now."

"I'm on it," replied the Radioman. He found the USS Alaska listed on the communications display and tapped on it with his finger to place the call.

A couple of fake ring tones later, Chrissie picked up the headset and answered the call. "Uh, hello, this is the Alaska. Chrissie speaking."

Still distraught after watching his father perish in an undersea struggle, Captain Connery staggered over to the communications panel and put Chrissie on speaker.

"Chrissie, this is Captain Connery on the USS Omaha Beach," the Captain announced. "What is your status?"

"Wow, you've been rescued," Chrissie replied to the message with delight. "Is everything okay?"

"Far from it," said the Captain. "We need to make a quick getaway. The Underworlders are not too happy with us at the moment, so we need to put some distance between us and them."

"What's an Underworlder?" Chrissie asked.

"I'll explain later, just pull a Crazy Ivan and make your way to the surface on an easterly course at flank speed," answered the Captain curtly.

"Sorry. I don't know who Crazy Ivan is. Can you please send Admiral Connery back over to us so he can tell us what to do," Chrissie replied. "We're mostly a bunch of kids over here, so we'll probably need his help."

"My father didn't make it," replied the Captain. "He lost his life fighting off Underworlders so we could escape."

Chrissie put her head in her hands and sobbed quietly for a moment. "The Admiral is dead," she announced to everyone in the Alaska control room.

The Alaska crewmembers and children were stunned and looked back at Chrissie in disbelief.

Back on the Omaha Beach, a teary-eyed Caroline embraced her father.

"You're going to have to do this on your own, Chrissie," the Captain spoke. "There's no more time to chat. I'm putting you in charge, so you need work with your friends and what's left of my crew and get the Alaska moving now."

Chrissie reached for the 1MC and broadcasted the news of the rescue and Admiral's death to everyone else on the sub. A mixture of somber faces, joy and outright crying erupted throughout the Alaska as everyone listened to the news.

Seconds later, she pushed the talk button on the 1MC microphone and announced:

"This is Chrissie and I'm taking command of the ship," she spoke with a wobbly voice. "Annie, bring us right to course zero-nine-zero and give me flank speed."

"Bringing us to course zero-nine-zero, all ahead flank, aye," Annie repeated, steering to the starboard and twisting the engine order telegraph to flank.

Back in Maneuvering, the Eng quickly responded to the flank bell by bringing more steam from the reactor.

"Mike, start filling the ballast tanks with air and then jump into the Planesman seat to control the stern planes," Chrissie ordered.

"High pressure air is filling the tanks and I'm jumping in your old seat," replied Mike.

"Chief of the Boat, you have the Conn," Chrissie announced as the Chief entered the control room. "I'm taking over as Diving Officer."

"Yes, ma'am," the Chief replied.

The Alaska made a 180 degree turn and began to accelerate upward. The Omaha Beach tracked in behind the Alaska and followed. The crews of both subs began to feel a bit of relief as they pulled farther away from the slow-moving Underworlder vessel.

Just as everyone was settling in for a speedy evacuation, a muffled voice was heard unexpectedly over the 1MC speaker in the Alaska control room. "Hey, let me in."

"Who is this?" Chrissie asked through her microphone.

"I'm trapped in the escape trunk. Somebody get me out of here."

"Who knows how to operate the escape trunk?" Chrissie looked around the control room.

"I watched the Chief of the Boat help Nick and Caroline get in there," Mike replied.

"Perfect. Annie, hold Mike's stern planes steady while he checks it out," ordered Chrissie.

Mike bounded out of his seat and headed down the passageway to the escape trunk. Upon arriving, Mike pushed the intercom button to communicate with whoever was inside the trunk.

"Who's in there?"

"Please let me out," replied the unfamiliar voice.

Mike unlocked the hatch and spun the wheel until it started to open. Suddenly, he was knocked to the deck as the occupant inside lunged out of the escape trunk. As he picked himself up off the floor, Mike came face to face with a pair of glowing, ultraviolet eyes.

"Stupid boy, you never open the door for uninvited guests." The Underworlder dropped his scuba rebreather on the deck, raised his hand, and unleashed a wave of heat that sent Mike flying backwards down the passageway.

"Ahhhh!" Mike screamed as he slid across the deck with his sunburned skin and smoldering clothes.

Mike wasn't the only one feeling the pain. Looking up at the Underworlder, Mike could see smoke coming off the creature's skin. Finding the source of his discomfort, the Underworlder smashed the fluorescent light tubes above his head bringing complete darkness to the compartment.

"What's wrong with you? Can't handle a little light?" Mike taunted the creature.

"It's just like a sun-worshiping Overworlder to bring the light of a burning star beneath the sea. You'll pay for your insolence, boy." The Underworld began walking toward Mike using his biological night vision.

Remembering the glow stick his father gave him on the Delta pier, Mike quickly pulled it out of his pocket and bent it until it snapped. The Underworlder was almost upon him when the ultraviolet light of the glow stick began shining from Mike's outstretched hand. The creature immediately recoiled in fear and pain as its translucent skin began to sizzle.

Jumping to his feet, Mike pressed forward toward the monster using the glow stick as a torch.

"You're a scared child and I don't think you have what it takes to finish me off," the Underworlder goaded Mike as he backed into a corner.

"I might have been a boy when I set foot on this sub, but I'm a Underworlder slayer now! Eat this!" Mike jammed the glow stick into the Underworlder's mouth causing the creature to scream uncontrollably.

Mike grimaced as he watched the Underworlder's head turn into glowing cinders and then flake away as ashes on to the floor. Still in shock from what had just transpired, Mike was suddenly jolted back to reality as he heard the announcement over the 1MC speakers.

"Conn, sonar, the towed array is telling me that the large object to our stern is increasing speed and closing the distance between us." The intense heat of the diamond-shaped vessel propelled it ever more quickly toward the fleeing submarines.

Mike scrambled back to the control room as Chrissie ordered the Chief of the Boat to communicate this news to the Omaha Beach via their underwater messaging link.

Sonarman Timbers on the Omaha Beach replied to the Alaska through his headset. "Alaska, thanks for the heads-up. We've got our own sonar suite and it looks like our luck is going south. I'm picking up thirty surface contacts and three submerged ones in front of us. My computer has classified the three submerged contacts as Seawolf-class submarines and they're heading in our direction with their torpedo tube outer doors open."

In all the excitement of rescuing their fathers from the clutches of the Underworlders, the pre-teen crew of the Alaska and Omaha Beach had forgotten that they were fugitives from the United States Navy. The Abraham Lincoln battle group had arrived at the scene after following the source of the underwater explosion. Their intelligence officers had also been monitoring some of the message traffic between the Alaska and the Omaha Beach.

"Conn, Sonar, I hate to say it, but things have just gone from bad to worse," announced the Alaska Sonarman. "I'm now picking up twenty-four Mark-48 torpedoes heading our way from the three submerged contacts. Our own submarine fleet is here to destroy us."

"Sonar, Conn, how long do we have until impact?" Chrissie asked.

"About thirty seconds," replied the Sonarman.

"Omaha Beach, we're all about to be clobbered by two dozen torpedoes in less than thirty seconds," Chrissie announced over the open communications link with the Omaha Beach.

"You're going to get hit before we do, so I suggest you brace for impact," Sonarman Timbers replied.

As if things weren't bad enough, the tip of the Underworlder craft began to split open and a gauze-like substance streamed out of it toward the Omaha Beach. Everyone onboard the DSRV felt a jolt as the gauze wrapped itself around the propellers.

"I'm getting a warning light on the propulsion system," Nick said, staring at the control panel. "The propellers have stopped but the turbines are still trying to spin them."

"Kill the steam to the turbines so we don't burn out the system," replied the Captain.

Nick took the steam from the nuclear reactor offline and the Omaha Beach began to fall backward as the

Underworlder craft reeled it into its large mouth-like opening.

"Alaska, we're in big trouble back here," the Captain communicated. "It looks like the Underworlder pyramid is going to pull us inside. I don't think we're going to make it."

"Skipper, I don't think any of us are going to make it," replied the Alaska Chief of the Boat. "We're just seconds away from torpedo impact."

Crewmembers on the Alaska and Omaha Beach braced themselves against nearby bulkheads, said quiet prayers, and plugged their ears with their fingers. All those aboard the Omaha Beach watched the large display in shock as twenty-four dots closed on their position from one direction while their DSRV was being pulled in the opposite direction.

"Chief of the Boat, sound the collision alarm," Chrissie ordered on the Alaska.

As the alarm went off, everyone onboard the Alaska closed their eyes for what seemed like an eternity. After ten seconds of silence, the Sonarman opened his eyes and looked at his waterfall sonar display. "Conn, Sonar, the torpedoes swam right by us!" he exclaimed. "Chrissie, it looks like they're heading for the Omaha Beach and the Underworlder ship behind us."

Underworlder Pyramid

Onboard the Underworlder vessel, the Navigator's glowing eyes gazed upon her computer display with grave concern. "Captain, in addition to the two Overworlder subs that are trying to escape, I'm seeing three subs heading for us and two dozen smaller projectiles that look like they're only seconds away from reaching us."

"Bring the Heat," the Underworlder Captain commanded.

Invisible fingers of intense heat reached out from the Underworlder craft toward the incoming torpedoes. The tremendous heat confused the closest torpedoes and caused them to veer off-course. Other torpedoes began to melt.

Unfortunately for the Underworlders, it was too little, too late. Over a dozen more torpedoes kept coming and began to detonate all around the diamond-shaped Underworlder submarine. All in all, eighteen torpedoes found their mark and the vessel exploded into millions of crystal shards that sent an unprecedented shockwave through the ocean.

The Alaska, Seawolf, Connecticut, and Jimmy Carter submarines were tossed like toy boats through the ocean as the massive concussion reached them. In an instant, there were dozens of injuries as crewmembers who hadn't strapped themselves in were thrown around inside their respective submarines.

Mike flew out of his chair and slammed into a nearby control panel while Chrissie hung on to the periscope handles for dear life.

"Ahhhhh!" Mike yelled out in pain as blood ran down from the top of his head.

After stabilizing, each of the submarines except the Omaha Beach performed an "emergency blow" in order to rapidly reach the surface. Submarines flew out in every direction of the ocean in spectacular fashion. Naval frigates, destroyers and the USS Abraham Lincoln aircraft carrier were already waiting when the Alaska surfaced. A helicopter carrying a half-dozen Marines and the Rear Admiral in command of the Lincoln battle group flew out toward the Alaska as the giant submarine settled on the surface.

"Terrorists onboard the Alaska, you're surrounded," barked a Marine, holding a megaphone on the helicopter. "Disembark from the sub with your hands on your head."

The hatch from the aft escape trunk of the Alaska opened, and Mike, Annie, Chrissie, the Chief of the Boat, the ship's Engineer and other crewmembers climbed out and stood on the flat missile deck with their hands on their heads. Puzzled sharpshooters on the helicopter kept their M16s trained on the kids and the others.

"Admiral, those don't look like terrorists," one of the Marine gunners exclaimed. "Some of them look like kids."

"Stay alert, Marine," replied the Rear Admiral. "We don't know what we're dealing with yet. The real hijackers might still be below-decks hoping to avoid capture. It's go time."

Two ropes dropped from the helicopter and four Marines rappelled to the Alaska's missile deck. Three of the Marines pointed their guns at the group, while the Marine First Sergeant walked up to the Chief of the Boat.

"COB, I sure hope you're not mixed up in this," said the First Sergeant. "Stealing a Trident isn't going to look good on your next evaluation."

"I am most definitely mixed up in this," the Chief of the Boat replied. "I helped Admiral Connery and these kids find and rescue their fathers, no thanks to you."

"I don't see the Admiral in your little group of traitors," the First Sergeant retorted. "Where is he?"

"Well, first he transferred to the Omaha Beach and then he…"

"Shut-up, COB." The First Sergeant cut him off before he could finish his sentence. "I read the story in the Navy Times. The Omaha Beach was destroyed in an accident and the crew died with it. I'm no fool."

"That's not true," a sobbing Annie spoke up. "You're definitely a fool and you trigger-happy cowboys just destroyed the Omaha Beach with your torpedoes. Our dads were rescued only to die at the hands of the Navy they served and loved."

Annie, Mike and Chrissie clung to each other, as they cried over the deaths of their fathers and best friends.

"What's going on here?" the First Sergeant snapped.

Suddenly, the Omaha Beach burst out of the water next to the Alaska to the amazement of onlookers everywhere. Covered with hundreds of embedded shards of glass, the DSRV's top-secret, flexible titanium hull had protected it from the torpedo explosions. A few moments later, the forward hatch on the Omaha Beach opened, and Caroline, Captain Connery, and the rest of the missing fathers climbed out onto the deck and wings of the advanced DSRV. They began waving to the surrounding ships and helicopters.

"Those sailors and that sub aren't supposed to exist," the Sergeant thought to himself, as he looked at the group in disbelief.

Seeing this from the helicopter, the Rear Admiral from the Abraham Lincoln got on the radio and directed the lead destroyer to pull in between the Alaska and the Omaha Beach.

"Warrant Officer, put the chopper down on the approaching destroyer's helipad." ordered the Rear Admiral to the pilot. "Also, get a portable SEAL Magnaphone ready just in case I need to make some important satellite phone calls."

The Navy helicopter landed on the destroyer just as the ship came to rest between the DSRV and the Trident. After shutting down its rotors so everyone could hear, the Rear Admiral grabbed a megaphone, climbed out of the helicopter and turned to address the members of the Omaha Beach. "You all are supposed to be dead!" he called out bewilderedly.

"We had about given up on ever seeing sunlight again," Captain Connery yelled back to the Rear Admiral from across the water. "If it weren't for our brave kids and my father, we'd still be imprisoned on the ocean floor."

"Wait a minute, Captain," the Rear Admiral retorted. "Are you telling me that these kids and retired Admiral Connery stole one of the taxpayers' subs to come rescue you?"

"That's correct, Admiral. We're alive today because of their heroic actions," responded Captain Connery.

"Captain Connery, in light of their traitorous actions in stealing one of America's most important pieces of property, these kids are lucky to be alive," the Rear Admiral snapped back. "I've had the entire Pacific Fleet hunting them down with orders to sink the Alaska.

Caroline emerged from behind Captain Connery on the Omaha Beach and shouted, "Admiral, we had no choice. When the government covered up our fathers' disappearance, we were their only hope to make it back alive. If Granddad hadn't helped us, we never would've been able to rescue them."

"Whoa, so you think there's a big government conspiracy trying to suppress the truth?" the Rear Admiral quipped. "I didn't exactly land here in a silent black helicopter. Listen, I'm as thrilled as anyone to see Captain Connery and the rest of your dads still alive. What you don't understand is that the ends can't always justify the means. As the only adult involved in this matter, Admiral Connery will have to sort these things out at his Court Martial."

"That'll never happen; Caroline's Granddad is dead," Nick shouted across to the destroyer as he emerged on the deck of the DSRV. He had a heavily restrained, blanket-covered figure in tow behind him. "Admiral Connery was the bravest and most patriotic man in America. He died saving me, Caroline and the crew of the Omaha Beach from the Underworlders."

"Excuse me, son, did you say Underworlders?" The Rear Admiral had a perplexed look on his face.

"I'm not your son," Nick shot back defiantly. "Who did you think captured our fathers? Who did you think sank that cruise ship? Whose very existence needed to be kept secret so badly that the President of the United States would lie to our faces at Arlington National Cemetery and pretend our fathers were dead?"

"These creatures won't stop until every human being is dead." Caroline piped up. "The Navy had to know something like this might happen. Our fathers weren't taking part in some science experiment. The Navy sent them to find out what was going on at the bottom of the ocean and just threw them under the bus when things didn't go as planned."

"Don't blame me or the Navy for the mess you've gotten yourself into," the Rear Admiral retorted. "Not only did you and your friends steal a Trident, you now have to account for Admiral Connery's death. I'm not buying your fantasy story about Underworlder creatures as the cause of all these events or the Admiral's demise. It's time you all take responsibility for your poor judgment and stop putting the blame on these figments of your imagination."

"Oh yeah? Well, what do you think about this figment, Admiral?" Nick spun around on the deck of the Omaha Beach and yanked the blanket off the Underworlder's head to reveal a humanoid creature like nothing anyone had ever seen.

Sailors and Marines from every ship, submarine and helicopter looked on with a mixture of fascination and horror as the bald, translucent Underworlder began shrieking in pain as the sun's rays made contact with its skin. Through the excruciating agony, the creature stared at its new enemies with his ultraviolet eyes.

"God in Heaven," the Rear Admiral uttered. "Get me the President."

Subase Bangor

Two weeks had passed since Caroline and Nick had been out at sea on the deck of the Omaha Beach. Now the two of them were sitting in front of the large statue of Admiral Connery at the submarine base back in Washington State. There were flowers, lit candles and notes all around the base of the statue from those who loved and respected the famous submariner. Nick slowly pulled out a letter from his pocket and handed it to Caroline. The return address on the envelope was from the White House. She opened the letter and began to read:

Dear Caroline,

The letter you are reading now represents my private thoughts as President of these United States. I want to express my regret and sincerest apologies to you, Nick, your family and your friends for the ordeal you endured. I did, in fact, send your father and his hand-picked team to go investigate a disturbance at the bottom of the Pacific Ocean after a cruise ship had mysteriously disappeared. I covered up the circumstances around their disappearance, and for that I am truly sorry. As a direct result of my deception, the country lost a true hero, your grandfather, Admiral Connery.

You, Nick, your grandfather, your friends and your mothers took incalculable risks to their own lives and broke virtually every law on the books to rescue your fathers. Along the way, you all demonstrated a rare level of bravery, intelligence and resourcefulness in the face of obstacles few have ever encountered, let alone surmounted. When I think of you, I am reminded of the words of Sergeant John B. Ellery from the 1st Infantry Division after his D-Day experience on Omaha Beach back in 1944:

"You can manufacture weapons and you can purchase ammunition, but you can't buy valor and you can't pull heroes off an assembly line."

Caroline, you and Nick possess a level of valor without equal and you, your grandfather and friends are all American heroes. This country is eternally grateful for the three generations of Connery submarine warriors who have fearlessly defended us. You and Nick have conspicuously distinguished yourselves through gallantry at the risk of your lives, above and beyond the call of duty while engaged in an action against an enemy of the United States. I hereby award both of you the Medal of Honor, and your friends will all be receiving the Navy Cross.

You and your friends have discovered a previously-unknown species that wants to destroy all of mankind; but you've found their weakness and defeated them in the first battle between our two civilizations. As we enter into this struggle, we know our lives will never be the same. Luckily, this country has a secret weapon. That weapon is you, Caroline.

As a middle school student and a civilian, you might be wondering how you're able to receive the highest military honor our country has to offer. By executive order, I hereby appoint you, Nick, Chrissie, Mike and Annie to be Officers in the United States Navy. Don't worry about being too young to be in the Navy; over a hundred years ago, another special person was accepted into the Navy at age fifteen before finishing high school. His name was Chester Nimitz and he went on to become a Fleet Admiral who helped America win the conflict in the Pacific during World War II. You and your friends will fly to Washington, D.C., next week to be honored and to receive your awards for the entire world to see.

Last of all, I'm making you the Captain and Nick the XO of your own ship. The USS Omaha Beach now belongs to you. Your team constitutes an elite submarine force that represents our first line of defense against the Underworlders. You and your friends will still get to go to school and live as normal a life as possible; but when you are needed, your country will call on you.

I know this is a lot to take in all at once. Just take a deep breath and know that you have supporters all around this grateful nation to lean on and I'll always be your biggest fan.

Yours Truly,
President Harris

Caroline handed the letter back to Nick, tears streaming down her face. She stared longingly at the statue of her Grandfather.

"You didn't die in vain, Granddad. I'm just like you," she spoke aloud. "I'm a submariner and a proud American and you will always live on inside me. I'll serve my country just like you and my dad and I promise you – as long as I can still fight, these Underworlders will never defeat mankind!"

EPILOGUE

Deep within the Earth's crust, a uniformed Underworlder walked across the control room, carrying a slate device.

"Pharaoh, I have the battle report from our first encounter with the Overworlders," said the soldier.

"Give it to me," the Underworlder leader snapped, reaching out for the tablet. Upon reading the report, he crushed the device with his hands. "They will pay dearly for this!"

The soldier bowed in fear. "Is it time to unleash the volcanoes on the Overworlders?"

The leader of the Underworlders stared into the distance. "So let it be written. So let it be done."

ABOUT THE AUTHOR

A bestselling author of fiction and non-fiction books, Rob Tiffany has spent the last decade combining his military past with his high-tech present to take readers from the depths of the ocean to the world of mobile apps. Rob served with the Navy SEALs on a special ops delivery vehicle and patrolled the seas on a Trident submarine. As an Architect at the world's largest software company, he's in-demand as an advisor to executives and a speaker at conferences all over the world. He lives in the Pacific Northwest and you can learn more about him by subscribing to his blog at http://robtiffany.com and following him on Twitter at http://twitter.com/robtiffany.

Made in the USA
Charleston, SC
09 January 2012